Stardust's Journey

Written & Illustrated by
Helen Scanlon

Dedication

Mark McPartland was a kind and loyal friend to both horses and humans. *Stardust's Journey* is dedicated to his memory.

A friend is someone who shines a light when all around is dark—
I wanted to be that light. ~Stardust

Cover and book designed by Steven Scanlon,
Hampton, Connecticut
Cover illustration, Stardust ©2026 Helen Scanlon
Author photograph, Pines photograph (p.13), Moon photograph (p.102) by Steven Scanlon, 2024-2025

ISBN: 978-0-9894168-7-0

Foreword

When fellow Connecticut horsewoman and longtime friend, Helen Scanlon, asked me to write the foreword for her latest book, Stardust's Journey, I was thrilled. It is a unique, important story written from the perspective of the rescue horse. Hopefully, it will make people aware of the plight of rescue animals at auctions, and sadly all too frequently—the kill pen.

Seven years or so ago, on a cold and wintery day, I took a chance on a sad, shaggy dark bay pony in the number 10 pen. With time and training, she became the best little dressage pony, my daughter's best friend, and the face of our rescue, PJ's Ponies. That leap of faith turned into a magical journey, like that of Stardust. It is one of the best things I've ever done. It has helped to break the myth that all discarded animals are broken, dangerous, flawed, or not worthy. The reality is that most, if not all, have been abandoned or cruelly abused. We've gone on to rescue several ponies over the years. With time, patience, and love each of them have proven to be absolutely amazing. All of them have been placed in wonderful forever homes.

PJ and I have been able to experience this magical journey and now, with the help of Stardust and the other unique and wonderful characters in this book, you can, too.

It is an easy reading story appropriate for many ages. It describes the darkness but also uplifts with lightness. It carries an important message that I hope will increase awareness of the plight of these animals. Please donate, volunteer, foster, or adopt and start your own magical journey!

Keirsten Riccio, Co-Founder
PJ's Ponies

Table of Contents

If there is a day…

When you call out
And silence calls back

When you reach for a hand
And grasp at the empty air

When you want someone to care
And told it is not for you

When you want to know hope
And it eludes you again

Please know that within your soul
The pilot light still glows

All you need to do is choose
To see its brilliant blueness

A tiny flicker.

You can see it.

I know you can.

Look in a different direction.

Turn your head.

Look to the pine trees
Just outside your window.

With the moon framed among the branches

To see where hope still lives.

~HS
March 13, 2023

Chapter One
I Am Stardust

My name is Stardust. I am a horse with a white star on my face and white stockings on my legs. My mane and tail are a rich, glossy ebony. My coat is a rich earth-brown, almost black. I am a polite and charming horse because my mommy is—she gave to me all of my best traits. I am proud to be her son.

My mommy's name is Emma, a name of great beauty and kindness. It is a name that fits my mommy perfectly, for she is the kindest and most glorious horse in the whole universe.

My mommy and I live a good life now, but we didn't always. There was a time when my mommy wasn't sure she could protect me from a cruel end.

Let me explain.

I don't know what breed of horse I am because no one knows where my mommy came from. You see, I was in my mommy's tummy when she was abandoned at a horrible place called an auction. My mommy told me it was a place where horses go when their humans can't take care of them—and sometimes they leave the auction on something called the Bad Truck—a huge metal monster that takes horses to the worst place of all; a place from which horses do not return. The auction is called the Bad Place by horses and the human rescuers. It is a place filled with tears and panic.

It is a place where hope struggles to survive.

My mommy never knew why our humans abandoned us and left our fates to simple luck. She just knew that one day they put her on a trailer, her pregnant tummy gently swaying side to side, and just left her at the Bad Place without even saying goodbye. She never saw their faces again.

My mommy remembered how I thrashed and kicked from deep within her, as if I knew that we were in grave danger. It was then that my mommy knew she had to save us. The instinct of the alpha mother mare was stronger than all of the steel gates and pens that kept us far from hope, frantic and desperate. My mommy's strength was like a fire that burned even when it rained. Her soul glowed red in her determination to find hope, even in this desperate place. She had to be sure we would not find ourselves on the Bad Truck.

My mommy told me she was scared at the auction, but she knew she had to be brave for me. She knew she had to save her baby, me—her only child.

My mommy was confused, terrified and very, very sad—her heart raced and her breath was quick, and at times she felt she would drop from exhaustion. She allowed her mind to be still and focused on what she needed to do to keep us alive. She chose courage. Courage is what would save our lives.

She also told me that she stayed sweet so a human would see her and take her to safety. My mommy's huge liquid eyes locked with every human who passed by our pen, pleading with them to help us. If she could reach out and touch a human with her soft muzzle, she did. A few humans stepped back when she did that, fearful that she would bite them. But that did not dampen her determination to find hope amongst the humans.

Her strategy proved to be successful: some nice humans spotted my mommy in a cramped, filthy pen with a number painted on her hip and approached her. My mommy reached out with her nose to gently touch the humans and told them with her energy that she needed a home. One woman gently stroked my mommy's face when she nuzzled her. My mommy pressed her head into the human's touch.

My mommy's strength came from kindness. She never used her teeth or hooves to hurt any living being, and the woman saw a special horse in my mommy.

I have a baby inside of me—please help us, she said to the woman as she explored her pockets for apple slices.

How she had missed apple slices and kind words. Maybe this human had some of both? To her delight, she did. The apple, a mesmerizing deep red with swirling light-green patches, sparked memories of a happier time when she ate sweet feed and grazed on grass and clover. The hope of tasting their richness again cradled her fearful heart.

When my mommy entered the auction arena, the sound was sharp and deafening. But she stayed strong and did not let the chaos change her course. Humans were crowded in the bleachers surrounding the arena and the whole scene smelled of burnt tobacco and fear.

The auctioneer bellowed as loudly as an angry goose, and I kicked deep within my mommy's tummy to let her know how frightened I was of his voice. It was not a soothing voice; it was rough and hurried and without a hint of warmth.

My mommy stood quietly in the middle of the arena to show the potential buyers how gentle she was. Her hope was that she reached the eyes and heart of the woman she had recently nuzzled. Was she among the crowd bidding on the discarded horses? Was she there to save her and me from the Bad Truck?

She was.

The soft-spoken human with the apples bid on my mommy and saved both of us. Soon after, my mommy felt the roughness of a nylon halter cradle her tired face. That halter meant that she was leaving the Bad Place. She welcomed it.

My mommy eagerly walked up the ramp of the kind woman's horse trailer and was met with a full hay net. She devoured mouthful after mouthful of the crunchy hay stalks and let it fill her empty and rumbling stomach. My mommy was so very hungry—and so was I. I stopped kicking from inside of her tummy when the nourishing energy of the hay reached me.

At last, she was away from the auction—the Bad Place. We were safe, we were not to go on the Bad Truck. My mommy fluttered a deep exhale from her nostrils as the trailer drove far away from the auction with the forgotten horses. The trailer took us to a place called Summerbrook Stables, a farm with lots of other horses and more kind humans. Summerbrook was to become my first home.

One beautiful early morning, just as the sky turned orange and pink, I was born at Summerbrook. The first human I ever met was a caring lady named Heather. I remember she smelled of sugar and tea leaves and had a calm and steady voice that was not at all like the auctioneer's bellow. She was the kind human who had loaded me and mommy on the trailer and took us away from the Bad Place.

Heather helped my mommy bring me into the world, and after I plopped onto the straw with my long legs jumbled every which way, I remember her gently holding my head in her hands and telling me how handsome I was.

"A colt," she whispered in my ear. "A handsome, perfect colt with a star."

I remember my mommy licking me dry and fussing over me to make sure I was healthy and strong. My newborn heart was strong and my spirit glimmered like silver. The Bad Place had not left its fearsome mark on me.

Heather named me Stardust because of the perfect white star in the center of my face.

My mommy and I stayed at Summerbrook for a short while, and after I grew up a little and became stronger, it was time for us to go to our forever home with a new human family.

We have a new farm to go to, my mommy explained to me. *They will take care of us there. Heather made sure of it.*

I remember the day I was brought to my new home. It was a clear spring day with lots of puffy clouds sweeping the sky. I was sad to leave my friends at Summerbrook Stables, especially my friend Magic, the kind chestnut Arabian gelding who was a treasured school horse. The day mommy and I left, he had whinnied a long goodbye to me as the truck and trailer started its journey down the winding, gravel-dotted Summerbrook driveway:

Be brave, young Stardust! I will always remember you!

Of all of the wonderful horses and humans at Summerbrook, I was going to miss Magic most of all. He was funny and smart, and he liked to tell me how fast and strong I was. He even liked to play with me. He was the only grown-up horse who did and the gesture made me feel special and loved. Magic was my first friend, and I knew I would never forget him either. He taught me that friends make our lives rich and whole, and that true friends believe in us and want us to be happy.

Even though I was but a baby, I knew I would never see Magic again. I knew he would want me to be brave, so I tried my hardest even though I was frightened by the loud clanging of the trailer as it bumped its way down the road away from Summerbrook. I heard Magic's whinny grow fainter, and fainter still:

Goodbye, Stardust!

Be brave, Stardust!

Remember me, Stardust!

I will always be your friend!

I will miss you and think of you!

His loud, trilling song was a bittersweet farewell.

I steadied myself on my mommy's flank as the trailer went over potholes and bumps in the country roads. She always stood strong and still and I felt completely safe when I had her to lean on.

I am scared, Mommy, I nickered nervously to her. My voice was small.

Just then, the trailer slammed into a particularly deep pothole. Every beam and joint creaked and rattled alarmingly, but my mommy told me that we were okay. The sound of clanging metal was oddly familiar to me, even though this was my first time in a trailer not being in my mommy's tummy. My heart raced like a rabbit's from deep within my chest as I stood firm, swaying with the movement of the trailer.

Nothing to be scared of, sweetness, my mother reassured me. *Elaine and her daughter Kris love horses, and I hear they have a big barn and lots of open, grassy fields.*

I breathed in deeply, flaring my little nostrils to drink in the chilly springtime air. I let the air fill my lungs to the very bottom, and my heart beat just a little slower. I felt my mother's warmth against my cheek, and it gave me a smile.

If my mommy is with me, I can do anything, I thought. I let the words comfort me. There was nothing to be afraid of, just like my mommy promised.

After our ride in the trailer, which was thankfully somewhat short, my nervousness gave way to excitement. The air, still chilly, had a new energy contained in it—it was the energy of my safe future and it embraced my being like a soft blanket.

What new adventures await me, I wondered. As long as my mommy was close by and watching over me, I could be as brave as I wanted.

The first human voice I heard came from Elaine, the owner of our new home. It was deep and earthy, like she had been working on a farm her whole life, and it was pleasing to my young ears.

"Hello, Emma and Stardust!" She said to us. "Welcome home to Faraway Hill!"

My mommy instinctively nickered at Elaine's kind voice. So, I copied her and did the same.

"Oh my gosh, you are so cute, Stardust," Elaine said with a little laugh.

Then, another human voice joined in—it was Kris, Elaine's daughter.

"Nothing cuter than a baby nicker," Kris said as she exited the truck. She had driven us to our new home, our new safe place. Her voice was slightly higher than Elaine's, and it reminded me of the sound of rainfall. It was gentle and soothing and made my heart feel as if it was wrapped in sunlight. I let her voice warm my trembling insides until I was no longer afraid.

The creaky steel gate of the trailer slowly swung open—its hinges making a high-pitched whistling sound that made me twitch my ears—and my mommy and I got our first glance of our new human family. I put my little baby nose in the air and took in deep breaths of all of the new smells of my new home. The aroma of alfalfa, sugar, and pine sawdust mingled together to help me form a lifelong memory. Elaine and Kris both stood quietly smiling at us, and cooing at how cute I was. Their clothes were dusty and frayed from years of barn work, and hay and sawdust were permanently embedded in the fibers. Their smiles were wide and warm as they approached us with a calm confidence.

My mommy nickered again when Elaine snapped a lead rope to her halter.

"Didn't I tell you how nice and trusting this mare is?" Elaine told Kris as she patted my mommy's neck. "Emma grabbed my heart the minute I met her, look at her—she is just so sweet even after all she has been through."

"Amazing that someone just threw her away," Kris said. "She is such a good-mannered mare. She practically hopped on the trailer like she knew. How could she have ended up pregnant at auction—heartbreaking."

My mommy carefully followed Elaine down the ramp and off the trailer, being mindful of each footfall and not losing sight of me. I followed close behind and grabbed a few strands of my mommy's tail in my mouth so I didn't lose her.

I am right here mommy, don't walk so fast, I told her.

The solid ground was firm under my hooves and it was a welcome change after being rocked back and forth in the noisy trailer for many dusty miles. It felt so good, in fact, that I kicked up my heels a little as I stayed close to my mommy's side. My legs were aching to stretch and full-out run, but I knew I had to stay close to my mommy. I was never far away from her.

"He's a little spitfire," Kris laughed. "Stardust!"

"Yes, that's what Heather named him," Elaine answered. "But feel free to change it since this guy will be your new project."

"Oh, he looks like a Stardust," Kris said as she rubbed my head. I playfully snorted and shook my ears at her touch. Her hand was unrushed and gentle. Her energy told me she was going to be a part of my life forever, and that made my heart flutter like a fledgling learning to fly.

"Heather picked a good name for him, I will keep it. He has a curious and twinkly personality," she added. "It fits him. My brave little Stardust."

My heart leapt like a cricket when she called me brave. She could see that I had the courage to ride in the big-horse trailer and not be scared. Magic, back at Summerbrook, knew I was brave, too. If Kris recognized bravery in me, then she was my friend, just like Magic. The energy at my new home felt safe and sure. The humans here were happy and I trusted them.

That night as my mommy and I lay down in our roomy stall piled high with sweet-smelling pine shavings, we counted all the things we were grateful for:

I am grateful to have my son with me, healthy and strong, my mommy said.

I am grateful to be here with you, Mommy, I said.

I am grateful we have food to eat and nice humans looking out for us, my mommy added.

I am grateful that this stall is soft and fluffy so I can curl up and sleep because I am tired from our long day, I added.

Sleep now, my Stardust, my mommy softly whuffled to me. Her breath was warm and smelled of molasses. She let out a long, whooshing breath as she settled into the bedding.

And with that, my mommy kissed the star on my forehead as she told me she loved me. I felt her breath tickling the tufts in my ears as I fell asleep, all warm in my bed. Home was a safe place.

I had many happy dreams that night.

Chapter Two
Growing Up

My early days at Faraway Hill were filled with fun, new friends and long days rolling in the cool grass with my mommy nearby. Our pasture was always dotted with butterflies skimming over the clover tops, and the sky above us was ever-changing and magnificent. How could the sky be so big, I often wondered. It held clouds and sun and rain and sometimes big, floaty snowflakes that settled on my long eyelashes. The sky could be bright one minute, then dark the next. Then, at night the sky went away. My mommy told me the sky was still there, it was just sleeping. Sometimes, I could see the moon when I looked out of our stall window. I was especially excited when I could see the stars glittering in the moon's orbit—because I was named after them.

There are the stars, my mommy told me. *They are powerful and beautiful, just like you.*

I also learned more about the other horses who lived at my new home. Kris was a horse trainer by trade, and she had two horses, Tara and Nala, before I came along to be her third.

Tara was a tall and elegant dark-bay mare who also befriended my mommy. She had always wanted to be a mommy herself, so she adopted me and became my second mommy. My mommy enjoyed Tara's company in our pasture and appreciated Tara's help in keeping an eye on me as I often played and leaped about, not minding where I would land. It was as if my hooves had hummingbird wings!

Be careful and don't run too close to the fence, Tara warned as I galloped around our pasture, circling my mommy and kicking out. I would let a squeaky little snort each time I sent my little hooves skyward. My youthful antics made Tara frantic with worry:

Don't kick up too high and hurt yourself, she fretted.

Sometimes, I got really hyper just to make Tara nervous. It was a super-fun game that entertained me no end: I would tear around the field snorting and kicking up clods of grass and dirt—then, I'd rear up and leap out with all four feet off the ground, land, and gallop off and stop just short of the electric fence.

Oh! Oh! Stardust, please DO be careful! she called out. *The fence bites!*

My mommy thought that was delightfully naughty of me—and Tara loved her job as babysitter. My mommy knew that Tara couldn't help herself, so she let her worry over me and take care of me as much as she wanted because she knew it made Tara happy. My mommy knew I was safe and just having fun—even if my legs went every which way.

Now, allow me to tell you about Nala.

Nala was a gray mare who was quite different from Tara. She seemed annoyed by me; laying her ears back in disgust anytime I was anywhere near her space. She was also wary of my mommy, so Elaine and Kris kept us in separate fields.

I asked my mommy why Nala didn't like me. It made my heart hurt because all I wanted was to be friends with her. It was odd that she seemed to dislike me, but Tara absolutely loved me. How could they be so different? Did I do

something wrong to Nala to make her not want to be my friend?

Not all horses have a feeling of safety in their hearts, some are scared and need time to trust, my mommy explained.

Am I a bad colt? Is that why she doesn't like me? I asked, my voice shaky and unsure. I knew my mommy heard the hurt in my little baby voice when I asked my question.

You are a very, very good colt, my son. You are sweet and polite and respectful of others. Her feelings toward you have nothing to do with you and everything to do with her, my mommy replied, offering me comfort and reassurance.

I took it gladly because my insides were heavy with sadness.

But my mind was not still. So many things I needed to know. I asked my mommy to explain more to me:

Why does Nala put her ears back when she sees other horses?

When Nala puts her ears back, it is because she is scared. She has been hurt by humans and bossed around by bigger and stronger horses, so she doesn't trust others, my mommy gently explained.

Be patient with her and send her your happy energy. Your kindness could help her break through her fear so she trusts you, my mommy continued.

Sometimes we just need someone to give us time and truly listen. You must remember to not crowd her. Let her come to you. And always, always be kind.

My mommy was wise and patient. I listened closely to every word.

The next time I saw Nala she was being led out to her field. She was turned out all by herself and I thought that was sad—wasn't she lonely?

When Kris unclipped the lead from her halter, Nala slowly walked off and dipped her head and grabbed big mouthfuls of grass, not pausing to chew thoroughly before stuffing her face with more. She ate as if she would never see grass again.

I stood by the fence of my field and watched her from afar. Tara and my mommy were nearby grazing—both had an eye on me because they knew that by watching Nala I could make her snort and stomp with anger.

It was then that I decided to send kindness out to Nala. I knew that when anger met kindness, kindness always won. My mommy had taught me that.

Hi Nala, I said simply, sending my energy on the gentle wind that ruffled the tips of the grass in her field.

Then, the air was still. I sent her another message:

My name is Stardust.

Leave me alone, I am eating, she shot back. *Don't eat my grass. I am hungry.*

Her energy glowed a bright orange-red and I immediately felt her fear. Nala was a horse who had been hungry many, many times and the cold and lonely memory of hunger lived within in her still.

I am sorry, Nala, I replied. *I like eating, too. My mommy lets me eat grass because I am growing up to be a big boy. I won't eat your grass, I promise.*

I didn't know what else to say; I felt so silly and baby-like telling her that I liked eating grass. Of course horses liked eating grass. I just wanted us to have something in common. I wanted her to trust me.

Nala went silent as a winter night, but her energy softened oh-so slightly. The orange-red glow turned a golden-pink that flickered around the edges. Did my energy help her furious heart stop racing? Was this kindness working its magic?

She had heard enough from a young and curious colt full of questions. I let her be.

My energy floated in the air above her swirling like a light summer cloud as she continued to grab fiercely at the grass around her hooves, crushing the stems with her big teeth.

I let my mommy's wisdom guide me: *don't crowd her and always, always be kind.*

Chapter Three
Tara

Tara was Kris's top show horse. She was trained in the upper levels of dressage and as a team, they consistently garnered high scores at shows. Dressage is an equestrian discipline that requires both horse and rider to move in harmony in an elegant dance—every movement balanced and correct. It is beautiful to watch and looks much easier than it is. Dressage requires many years of training to achieve almost perfection and Tara loved performing dressage movements. She lived to make Kris proud.

She explained it to me like this:

I get to be fancy and lift my legs like I am dancing. When Kris is on my back I hardly feel her. All she needs to do is shift her weight or move her fingers on the reins and I know exactly what to do. It is so much fun! People clap for me and pat my neck and tell me how gorgeous I am. I love that!

When could I do something like that, I wondered.

Tara came to Faraway Hill when she was barely a year old, a little older than I was at the time. She had a fancy mother and a fancy father from another country across the wide and vast ocean. Tara was fancy, too—but she had no ego, and did not boast of her talent. She had a humble, generous soul and she simply loved making people happy. Tara had been treated with kindness from day one—she never knew fear or hunger, only soft words and gentle hands. She knew nothing of auctions, as it should be. No horse, or human for that matter, deserved to be mistreated. Tara was treated like royalty at Faraway Hill, because she truly was. She was an example for all horses to follow—love and respect your rider, follow them, please them, be willing to try new things. But also, let them know if something hurts or feels wrong. A good human will stop the ride, remove the saddle, and examine the source of the discomfort. A human's job is to take care of us. And horses, in turn, will take

care of our human. It is a harmonious partnership—a joyful friendship—that gives color to every day.

I could see in Tara's glistening brown eyes that her partnership with Kris made her life vibrant and joyful. Tara greeted each morning with a smile and perked ears, for she knew that her friend Kris would arrive at the barn soon with a kiss, a cookie, and a flake of sweet hay.

This was a natural way of being for her. It inspired every horse and human in that barn to live each day with an open heart and a curious mind.

And, we learned from her that if we perked our ears just so, we would also get a kiss on the nose from Kris.

Chapter Four
Nala

Now, allow me to share the story of my friend Nala. From what she told me—and from conversations in the barn aisles—I was able to piece together her life's journey. Nala was forthcoming with her tale—as difficult as it was. She told me, while holding back her soul-consuming sadness, hat that one day, she was a spirited filly playing by her mother's side, the next she was a grown-up horse and a feisty one at that. Nala hardly remembered her young and joyful days because she had been betrayed by humans early in life, and she nearly lost all hope—until one day…

But, that story is a sad one, so I shall start with how she came to know Faraway Hill as home.

Nala came to Faraway Hill by way of a local woman who bought Nala sight unseen for her young horse-loving daughter. Nala was barely a grown-up and mostly untrained, and the woman thought she and her daughter could learn together. The woman did not know that horses, especially young horses, required training to help them learn how to live happily in the human world.

It was a grave mistake that Nala paid for with her spirit.

The woman had soon discovered that although Nala was beautiful and moved like a swan on the water, she was not a kid's pony. Nala scared her daughter by being pushy, showing her big teeth and threatening to bite when she was scared. The woman's daughter grew more and more fearful of Nala, and soon stopped spending any time at all with her. The woman and her daughter had no idea what to do with Nala, and had no money for a proper trainer.

Unable to afford a trainer, the woman made Nala live alone in a small, grass-less paddock in the family's backyard. She was unhappy, fearful, and without purpose or friends. The woman and her daughter never visited Nala to try to

win her trust, they just threw hay over the fence and filled her water bucket. They didn't even say anything to her. Soon, Nala's light dimmed—her eyes lost their sparkle and she became angrier with each passing day. She wondered to herself:

Did I do something so terrible to deserve being tossed away like a rag? Why won't they help me? Why won't they feed me more? I am still young and I need lots of food!

Nala greeted every day with loneliness. She sighed with hopelessness when the sun rose over the horizon to illuminate the slick mud and piles of manure that clogged her paddock because that meant another day of dampness and endless hunger. Her water bucket was tinged with ever-present filth, never to feel the cleansing stiffness of a scrub brush. Her hay was reedy and brown, and although it was better than nothing, it was flavorless and left her feeling hungry—no matter how much she stuffed her jaws with it, her belly always felt empty. Her ribs started to protrude from her sides. Her itchy flanks never felt the bristles of a curry brush and a myriad flies swarmed around her constantly, driving her mad with their painful bites and stings.

One cloudy day, a day that Nala would never forget, Kris discovered her when she drove by the woman's home and saw the mare standing nearly ankle-deep in mud in a tiny paddock in the backyard. Kris pulled her car over to get a better look.

Kris stepped out of her car and called out to Nala, "Hey pretty mare! Hello, sweetheart!"

Nala snapped her head up like a puppet on a string and looked directly at Kris, and their eyes locked. Something inside of Nala told her to whinny back at the nice human with the soft voice:

Help me, I hate it here!

Kris heard the painful desperation in Nala's frenzied plea and it froze in an icy trail through her heart and down her spine. For Kris, seeing an animal in a desperate situation physically hurt her—it was a hurt so palpable that it always pushed her into action.

Kris saw that the mare was beautiful—skinny and dirty—but beautiful nonetheless. Nala attempted a weak trot in her little paddock so Kris could see how she moved. Kris clearly saw Nala's elegance and power in her muddy limbs—no sign of lameness—and was moved to utter a barely audible "wow." Nala moved like a dressage horse—floating and forward, even in a muddy cramped paddock—and even with a broken spirit. She was young, and even in her underfed state, she still had the flame of the alpha mare flickering within her. Kris watched Nala with the trained eye of a skilled horse trainer: this mare had potential and Kris wanted her. It was that simple.

Just think of what this mare could do in a dressage arena, Kris thought.

But, would her owners let her go?

Kris gathered her thoughts for only a minute before she found herself walking up to the woman's rundown house and knocking on the door. Kris was a determined human, and often acted on her first impulse of kindness, especially when an animal in need could not wait another minute to receive care. Many horses, dogs, cats—and even baby birds—were saved by her quick thinking and generous heart. That's my Kris.

She had to help this sad gray mare with the mud-caked coat and protruding ribs. It would be wrong to drive by and not do something. Kris knew that she would not be able to sleep that night if she didn't at least try.

The woman opened the door to find Kris practically begging her to let her take the downtrodden mare.

"Hello, my name is Kristine Jenkins and I drive by your place at least once a week—I never noticed her before now—but I would like to buy the gray mare in your back paddock. Please let me have her and name your price," Kris said assertively—and added a smile to soften her approach. She had already made up her mind that she was not leaving until she had the right answer.

The woman, stern and seemingly annoyed with Kris's persistence, didn't put up a fight—especially when Kris took out her checkbook. The woman wanted the mare out of her life.

"I am a horse trainer at Faraway Hill the next town over," Kris continued. "She will have a good home. I would like to buy her off of you, today."

The woman stood in the doorway, unsmiling, and kept the door mostly closed so as to not let Kris see the inside of her cluttered house. Kris smelled caustic cigarette smoke escaping from the partially opened door. When the smoky stench hit her nose it nearly made her take a step back. Kris held firm, though—there was no stepping back from saving Nala.

"Name a price," Kris pleaded, her eyes locking with the annoyed woman bracing the front door.

"I don't know why you'd want Nala. She has given us nothing but trouble. She bites, she kicks. She bucks riders off. She is a bad one, a rogue. She's all yours, good luck—I will pray for you that she doesn't kill you," the woman said impatiently.

"She looks like she needs me," Kris said simply, her steady rainfall voice never faltering.

"Do you have $500?" the woman asked. "Write me a check and she's yours. But I want that horse out of here today. Don't expect me or my daughter to help. That mare would kill us if she could. She is bad and dangerous."

Kris just offered a smile and said nothing, although there was much she could have said. Kris chose carefully when to give her energy—and in this instance, her energy would have been wasted. There was no teaching moment to be had here, it would only be met with anger. She just had to save Nala; it was her sole purpose on that day.

Kris took a pen out of her jacket pocket, and fished her checkbook out of her bag. Kris wrote out the amount on the check and hurriedly signed her name.

"I writing this check to…?" Kris asked.

The woman curtly told Kris her name, and spelled it so Kris could complete the check.

"Here is a check for $500, I will be by with a trailer in an hour," Kris said as the woman greedily snatched the check from Kris's hand, the ink still wet on the embossed paper.

"Fine, and like I said—we won't help you. You can back up the trailer from the side driveway, I'll open the gate for you. Make sure you are packed up and out of here within an hour of you getting here," the woman sneered before closing the door a little too abruptly.

Kris stood on the welcome mat feeling the breeze from the slammed door lightly lifting several strands of her hair. With a triumphant exhale, she walked away from the slammed door, got in her car, and laughed to herself as she put the key in the ignition. The engine started up with a triumphant rumble. She put the car in gear, and drove back to Faraway to fetch the truck and trailer, feeling like a little kid who just won a pony in a raffle.

As she ran in the barn to get the truck keys, she saw Elaine mucking stalls and told her mother that she had just paid a rude woman $500 for a starving mare kept in her backyard.

"Mom, you wouldn't believe this horse, she is amazing," Kris explained, slightly out of breath as she rushed around to get the truck and trailer ready. "She is starving—she is all ribs—but she still has a fire within her. She is amazing, she needs us."

"Well, go get her!" Elaine exclaimed without hesitation. "I will get a quarantine stall ready."

"Thanks, Mom," Kris said with a beaming smile. Her mother always supported her in times like this.

Kris kept her promise and arrived at the woman's home with a horse trailer to save the neglected mare. As she carefully backed down the muddy path to the Nala's paddock, the mare regarded the truck and trailer with cautious curiosity; ears perked and eyes wide. Kris exited the truck, and gently shut the truck door so she didn't startle Nala. Every move Kris made was gentle, quiet, and slow. This mare would know no more trauma.

Nala did not move as Kris approached her. She stood her ground, but was willing to share her space with Kris. Kris did not crowd her. Soon, Nala reached her nose out to touch Kris's well-worn canvas jacket sleeve, and explored the rough material with her muzzle. To Nala, the jacket smelled of hay, earth, grass, and sunshine and she opened her nostrils wide to breathe in the warm farm scent. It was an infinitely pleasing aroma to the mare who had only smelled mud and manure for many, many months.

Kris moved in closer to softly touch the mare's neck to pat it reassuringly. She discovered that Nala's dappled gray coat was matted with dirt swirls; her tail and mane were gnarled and twisted and filled with spiky burrs. Her hooves were overgrown and cracked and dry as sand.

Nala's eyes flashed a fiery red when Kris started to slip a thick nylon halter over her head. The mare pulled back and snorted with alarm when the halter touched her.

"Naaaaala, Naaaala, easy girl," Kris said soothingly as she lowered the halter, removing it from her face. "It's okay, it's a halter, it won't hurt you. I won't hurt you."

Nala snorted again at Kris, but lowered her head, allowing Kris to put a reassuring hand on her trembling neck. After more soothing words, Kris placed the halter over her head again, this time Nala allowed Kris to pull it over her ears and clip the buckle on the cheek.

"Naaaallllaaaaa," Kris said again, allowing the vowels in Nala's name flow over the mare like clear water.

Nala lowered her head and blinked slowly as Kris's fingernails gently scratched under her itchy, burr-gnarled mane.

"Naaaalllaaaa, sweetheart," Kris said, her rainfall voice barely above a whisper. "You want to come home with me? Would you like that?"

At that moment, the skies opened up a little to let a soft drizzle fall over them as they stood in the muddy paddock. Kris kept the lead rope slack so Nala could sense she wasn't going to tug on her.

Nala's energy released in torrent of truth and desperation, and sent it through the lead rope to Kris's hand.

I hate it here. Please feed me, Nala's energy said.

Kris's hand received the mare's emotional plea like an electrical current coursing through a lightning rod. It flashed hot and pulsated like a live wire. Kris shivered.

After a moment, Kris reached over to rub one of Nala's ears. Kris broke the stillness with a promise:

"You will never see this place again. Do you like sugar?"

Kris reached into her pocket and offered Nala the cube of sugar that was hiding there amongst the pieces of baling twine and crinkly candy wrappers.

Nala hungrily scooped it up from Kris's palm, her overgrown whiskers twitching like crabgrass in the wind.

"There you are," Kris said softly as Nala hollowly crunched the cube in her cheek. "Wanna come home with me? I have a nice trailer with lots of hay. See?"

Kris, still keeping the lead rope slack, and pointed to the trailer that was backed up to the paddock, its ramp down revealing the full hay net within.

"There is your way out," Kris whispered in Nala's ear. "Just step on like a good girl, and we'll go."

Nala moved forward, ears up—and Kris walked right beside her, keeping a hand on her neck to let her know she was safe. Nala moved faster and faster toward the trailer and Kris kept up. Nala nearly cantered onto the trailer as if she knew a better life awaited her. She bounded onto the ramp, her powerful hindquarters propelling her to the promise of home. She knew that the trailer was there to save her and she did not hesitate to get herself on it.

"Good, good girl!" Kris said excitedly as she patted the mare's neck. Kris let the lead rope go slack again, and Nala buried her face in the hay net and joyfully ate and ate and ate. Kris saw that Nala was not only gorgeous, but she was very, very smart—and had an innate sense of self-preservation. This horse was special.

Nala didn't even notice the trailer moving as she ate her fill of the most delicious hay she had ever eaten. She was brought to Faraway Hill to a warm, soft stall and even more of that sweet golden-green hay. Her tense muscles dropped and she let out breath that flitted like a cardinal. Free.

In Nala, Kris did not see a scary beast with wild eyes—she saw a brilliant horse with a fearful heart who just needed time and patience. Kris saw Nala's long, graceful legs and natural balance—the advanced movements in dressage were in her future with the right training. Kris had worked with many "difficult" horses and knew exactly what to do to earn Nala's trust. It mostly involved giving Nala all the time she needed, but also giving her clear instruction on how she was to behave:

Do not use your teeth on humans. Do not lift your legs to kick at humans. Do not push humans around, they are smaller than you—be respectful.

Nala was a quick learner and soon she was not nipping at people as they walked by her stall. Soon after that, she was able to be led safely and wasn't pushy. Each time she did something correctly, she was showered with "good girl!" praise and cubes of sugar. It was as if Nala was waiting to be shown what was expected of her. When she received Kris's calm leadership, she soaked it up like the rays of the sun on an autumn day. Nala welcomed it. She had been waiting a long time for her purpose to make itself clear.

So this is what is right, she seemed to say. *This feels good.*

Nala had been ridden before so she knew how to carry a human, but she had not done it in a long time. And those rides before Kris were sloppy and unsafe with the human on her back rushing her, kicking her sides, and yelling at her to 'whoa' when she bolted. Nala had even bucked one of her riders off her back like an annoying gnat. That felt wrong to Nala and it distressed her greatly. She had not wanted to be a bad horse, she just wanted to get away from the pain inflicted on her by a careless rider. Nala did not want to hurt anyone but it seemed that no one listened unless she did something drastic. Even then, she could not find a way to let the humans in her life know that she wasn't being true to her nature.

I am a horse, her energy had cried out to her humans. *Please let me be who I am, and please don't hurt me.*

Kris knew that Nala was highly intelligent and with the right job, she would flourish. Kris was right.

The first time Kris put a saddle on Nala's back and climbed aboard, it was apparent: Nala wanted a job, and she wanted to do it well. She wanted to please Kris, the nice human with the rainfall voice and pockets full of sugar cubes.

Their early rides consisted of mostly Kris sitting lightly in the saddle and doing the basics in the riding arena. Walk, track left, halt, serpentine three loops, trot, walk, halt, twenty-meter circle to the left and the right, a little more trot, a few strides of canter....

Soon, Nala became strong and took to dressage like a dolphin riding an ocean wave. Her hoofbeats were light and balanced. Her spirit was as bold as a hawk circling the open skies; her nostrils flared with each breath as she surged forward in her gaits. She was a mare worthy of Epona, the goddess of horses.

Nala soared like a heron when Kris rode her: they would glide across the surface of the riding arena and not make a ripple. And, the wonderful thing was, when Kris rode Nala, Nala seemed almost....happy? When she performed dressage movements, Nala always had one ear cocked back to listen to Kris. Kris never asked Nala to perform something she couldn't do comfortably. As a result, Nala grew more confident every day.

Her purpose grew and became clearer with each ride. Nala had been like a rough-hewn piece of oak—with each new movement learned, the roughness smoothed out. Her muscles grew stronger and her mind became more focused.

Nala also adored Kris, it was evident every time Nala nickered for her and perked her normally laced-back ears at the sound of her voice. It was as if Nala was thanking Kris—and why not? Kris gave a lonely, forgotten horse a purpose; a reason to greet each morning with confidence and gratitude; a second chance to live a life full of joy.

Now, if she would only be my friend. But I knew Nala didn't have much experience with other horses and she was scared that they would hurt her because she had been bullied by some of them when she was young. I wanted her to know I was safe—that I would treat her with kindness so she could trust me. I knew that trust grows from kindness, and trust is what defeated fear.

Nala deserved a friend after all the loneliness she had endured. A friend is someone who shines a light when all around is dark—I wanted to be that light.

Chapter Five
Be My Own Horse

The days of my youth were joyous and fun—I played all day with my mommy (and Tara!) watching over me, I napped in grass and let the sun warm my back, and I raced the dragonflies that zipped around our field. My mind was free of worry as I grew stronger every day.

I knew that I was getting older—I ate grain, hay, and grass like the grown-up horses. I had my own halter and lead rope. I was trained to lift my hooves so they could be cleaned and trimmed.

You are getting to be a grown-up horse, my mommy told me. *Soon, you and I will live our separate lives. I am proud of you as you have done well to be polite and respectful.*

Why do we need to live apart from each other? I pleaded. *I like being with you every day.*

It is nothing to be sad about, my mother gently assured me. *It just means you are becoming your own horse with your own purpose. We will still both live here at Faraway Hill—and I will still see you. But soon you will be Kris's new riding horse.*

My mommy's unworried energy calmed my nervous heart. At least we would still live at Faraway Hill together! But, what would happen to those long, lazy days playing under the big, big sky? Would I still chase the butterflies with my mommy nearby watching over me? Would I still nap in the sun as she grazed? Would I still race the dragonflies? Would my mommy still kiss my star and tuck me in at night? Suddenly, my heart felt like it contained heavy stones. It hurt. I felt the tears form in my eyes as the stones made my heart even heavier. The stones pulled me down and dared me not to cry. I tried to blink the tears away and be brave, but they kept coming back—sharp like ice, but hot as flame. Finally, I let myself cry because I was sad and I wanted my mommy to know so she could help me.

Mommy, I want to still be with you, I cried. *I love you, Mommy! Please may I stay with you?*

My mommy craned her neck around mine as she softly spoke into my ear. She held me close as I sobbed my sharp, hot tears. I breathed in her warmth and it smelled like home.

My dear son, my mommy whispered. *It is not a sad time. You are a fine and elegant horse. Kris will take you to those big shows like she does with Tara. You will shine as bright as the stars you were named after. Growing up and learning is a reason for celebration.*

But, I will miss you, I sniffled.

I will always be right here, she said as she kissed the star on my forehead. *And I will always be proud of you. Always.*

I slowly closed my eyes as her energy enfolded me in its gentleness. The last thing I heard before I fell into a deep, dreamy sleep was my mommy nickering softly in my ear. Her voice was as soft as dandelion seeds, and it floated right into my being and offered safety.

I knew that this was the last time my mommy would tuck me in, even though she never told me it was. I was growing up to be too big to fit in a stall with her and, like she said, it was time for me to be my own horse. I was no longer scared because I knew that my mommy would always be at Faraway Hill, ready to celebrate my grown-up accomplishments with me.

I was still sad to say good-bye to my foalhood, and my tears were right at the surface, but I greeted adulthood with eagerness and wonder. I was to take a great adventure. I breathed in deeply. No more tears fell.

My mommy taught me to be brave because she was the bravest horse I knew. Yes, life moves forward—and the unknown can be scary—but we can choose to embark on our life's journey with a sense of wonder.

There was much beauty and joy in the world and I was ready to discover it.

Chapter Six
A Grown-Up Horse

My new stall was in another barn away from my mommy.

The day I was led away from her to start my own life, the sky was filled with puffy violet-gray clouds swollen with the promise of a storm. I felt the same as the clouds looked: sad and stormy. Just the day before I had felt so brave, now I felt like a baby again. I was confused. Was I actually ready to be a grown-up? I knew in my heart I was ready, but my love for my mommy was overwhelming me in a wave of sadness as reality sunk in: *I was a grown-up horse. No more mommy time.*

Kris held onto my lead rope with a strong but patient hand, and even though I was prancing and looking behind me to find my mommy, she never once impatiently tugged on the rope. When I trumpeted through my fluttering nostrils, she didn't shush me. She knew I needed to process my sadness and confusion in my own way—and she was right there, holding onto to me so I wouldn't be as scared. When my mommy whinnied back at me, I felt like breaking free to be with her. But I didn't pull such a stunt because I remembered what my mommy taught me: *always be polite and respectful.*

Mommmmyyyyyy! I called out.

I was frantic. I still wanted to be a baby; I didn't want to grow up. I surrendered to my sadness and willed my bravery away—I missed her so much already. I was scared to grow up. Maybe I wasn't ready? My mommy always took care of me. I never had to worry when I knew she was near.

Stardust! My mommy called back. *I am right here, just over the hill from your new barn. I am not far from you.*
I want to be a baby! I whinnied. *I want to be your baby! Who will tuck me in at night? I am scared!*

At that moment, I felt Kris's warm hand patting my neck.

"It's okay, sweetheart," she said to me in her gentle rainfall voice.

I soaked up her touch and it immediately eased my panic: *Kris. There is Kris. Kris is with me. I am safe.*

But, my mommy....

At that moment, my mommy called out to me:

You will always be my baby. Even when you are an old, old horse. I will always be your mommy.

Her voice was warm as a bran mash and sweet as a sugar cube. Her words held me in a loving embrace and it dulled the sharp edges of my fear and sadness.

Mommy.

Kris walked me into my new stall and unclipped the rope from my halter. The other horses in the barn peered over their stall doors with perked ears, curious about their new neighbor: me.

It was then that I heard Nala whinnying.

Is that Stardust? she called out from her stall at the far end of the barn.

Nala? I whinnied back. *I am scared!*

Don't be scared, Stardust! she said. *I know what it is like to be scared. You are okay!*

It was then that I knew my earlier kindness and patience with Nala had made an impact on her. My mommy was right. The way to make a friend is to be kind.

Nala, I don't want to grow up, I whinnied. *I miss my mommy.*

I know you miss her, Nala replied gently. *Let your mind be still. You are safe. Kris is your friend. And I am your friend.*

Nala's words flickered like the stars that surrounded the moon on an inky dark night. Her energy was peaceful and felt warm like my mommy's breath in my ear. I let my neck muscles relax and they released a torrent of tension that dissipated into the air of the barn. Nala was my friend because I was kind to her. She was being kind to me when I needed kindness the most.

And Kris was right there with me, her hand still on my neck, her soft voice comforting my fretful soul.

"Easy, sweetheart," she told me. "Easy, little man. Brave, brave little man. I know it hurts. You love your mommy, it's okay to miss her."

It was then that I leaned into Kris's rough canvas barn coat and let my tears flow like a summer rainstorm. With each drop that escaped my eyes, I became more my own horse. I knew I would forever love my mommy, but I was a grown-up. It was my time. Maybe this wasn't so bad. Kris was here.

In that moment, I was truly ready.

"There you go, my little man," Kris whispered to me as she caressed the itchy spot under my forelock. "There you go. We all love you. It's okay, it's okay. You just lean on me."

After that first day away from my mommy, Nala and I grew closer in our friendship. I discovered that she was not an angry horse at all, she was just scared because she had been neglected and discarded early in her life. This made her hesitant to trust anyone—horse or human. That day, Nala revealed that she was a gloriously compassionate horse with a heart as big as the sky above.

Once I won her trust, I could not have asked for a more loyal and caring friend.

Chapter Seven
The Strange Dreams

In those early days of my life, I had many troubling unanswered questions swirling in my mind. Where did I come from? Why was my mommy thrown away? Why was Nala neglected? Why did terrible things happen?

One question bothered me most of all: why do I feel like I was very close to not being where I am today?

Once I started asking these questions as a grown-up horse, I started having dreams that were both fascinating and terrifying. Some nights when I closed my eyes in slumber, vivid images occupied my brain in a myriad of colors and faces.

In these dreams, I could hear scared whinnying from nameless horses packed in small, dusty, spaces; knee-deep in manure. There were so many of them. Many were frightfully thin; some were quite old with clouds in their eyes and gray hairs on their faces. Some were panicked, some looked like they had simply given up. Some looked like my mommy. Some even looked like me. Who were these horses? Why were they in my dreams? What were they trying to say to me?

One dream in particular stands out as a revelation. In this dream, I felt like I was submerged in a pond, floating and confused—but I could breathe. I heard the whinnies of the nameless horses—but their frightened voices were muddled because I was in this pond. The whinnies got louder, and the pond started to roll and create waves. I was rocked back and forth as the waves in my pond got bigger and scarier. I felt trapped. The whinnies started to fade one by one as the nameless horses disappeared. Where had they gone? Why was I in water? Why can't I get out and save them—and save myself?

My questions were answered when the face of my mommy appeared in my dream. She was licking my face as I lay curled up in the straw at her feet.

I had been dreaming about my birth.

The pond had been my home inside of my mommy's tummy. The whinnies I heard were the horses from the Bad Place my mommy told me about: the auction.

I had heard those scared horses before I was born. Now, they were speaking to me when I slept.

My dream continued with my mommy telling me how lucky we were:

Our humans left us here. But we were saved by other humans with kindness in their hearts. Many of the other horses were not.

I woke suddenly from my dream, my coat slicked with sweat. My breathing was shallow and quick. All I heard were the noises of a still night—crickets, a faraway screech owl, the soft breathing of my sleeping friends in their stalls.

I cried silently to myself as I thought of the discarded horses at the auction. It was then that I realized that my mommy and I had been discarded too. We had been those scared horses.

I felt a deep and profound sadness grip me. It bit and stung and hurt me like deer flies in July. I cried more. I wanted my mommy so badly in this moment.

Stardust?

It was Nala's energy reaching out to me in the near-silent darkness.

Nala, I want my mommy, I sobbed. *I don't want to be brave anymore.*

Stardust, Nala said softly. *You don't have to be brave all the time. Sometimes we are scared. And it's okay. Just tell me what I can do for you. Friends can help when you are scared.*

Tell me I am safe and will never be in that awful place again, I cried.

You are safe. No one can hurt you, or your mommy, or me, Nala replied.

But I was a discarded horse before I was even born. How can I know that will never happen again? I pleaded.

I was discarded, too, Nala told me. *Just because we were thrown away early in life doesn't mean we will be discarded forever. It doesn't have to be our destiny. Now we are here at Faraway Hill. We live a life full of safety and love. And we will look out for each other. So will Kris. She will never let us go.*

What of the others? I asked. *I hear them in my dreams when I sleep.*

We can only send hope onto the wind for them, Nala said, a wisp of sadness in her voice. *We can wish for that hope to find them and hold them in love.*

Thank you Nala, I said to my friend. *I like talking with you. It makes me feel less sad.*

We don't have to be what the world first gave to us, Nala continued. *We can refuse to be discarded. We can fight and wish and move in the direction of hope. There is always hope. Always. Now, sleep dear Stardust. When the morning arrives, we will have a lovely breakfast and meet the new day with that hope in our hearts.*

Very soon after, I fell asleep in the deep shavings and let hope guide my troubled heart to a brilliant purple-skied morning.

Chapter Eight:
The Gentleman of Faraway

The first time I saw my mommy after being separated from her was such a glorious day; it reaffirmed what she told me: *I will always be your mommy.*

As soon as Kris unsnapped the lead rope from my halter to let me explore my new grassy paddock, I galloped to the far end to get a better look at her in the paddock next to mine—whinnying my joy all the while. My hooves tore up the grass and earth as my powerful limbs swiftly carried me. I felt as if I could fly in that moment.

Mommmmyyyyy! I trumpeted.

Hello, my dearest, my mommy whinnied back. *You look like you are doing wonderfully and growing up so strong!*

I am being brave, Mommy! I whinnied excitedly. *And Nala and I are friends!*

Of course you are, my mommy said proudly. *You are a kind and sweet horse. She knows she can trust you. You learned well.*

Tara was there, too—and she whinnied her gladness:

Oh sweet Stardust! We are both so proud of you!

I kicked up my heels and snorted my exuberance to show them how brave and strong I had become. I felt like a grown-up horse. My babyhood seemed so distant, so long ago. My dark coat glistened with a prism of midnight-blue, fire-red, and umber—and my eyes, wild and round—glowed with vibrant youth. My legs were as strong as timber; straight and sound. I was, as Kris called me, a magnificent horse with the heart of a lion.

Even though I grew big and powerful, I was gentle as a baby rabbit when humans tended to me, and I became known as the Gentleman of Faraway. I was surrounded by adoration, every day. The young humans who took riding lessons always stopped by my stall to pat my nose and comment on my beauty. I never used my teeth when they poked their small fingers through the bars of my stall—and I was careful when they offered me a sweet treat. My teeth were always hidden and never caused a human or horse to feel pain. My mommy taught me that.

"Hi Stardust!" the students said.

"He is so beautiful," they whispered.

"I wonder when Kris will ride him," they wondered.

I wondered that, too—I wanted to be a fancy riding horse like Tara and Nala and make Kris proud of me. Would I go to those horse shows like they did?

But for now, I was allowed to grow and develop before being asked to carry a rider.

Then, one bright and sunny morning after breakfast, I overheard Kris and Elaine talking about the day they would put a saddle on my back. It made my being spark with anticipation. A saddle meant I was a real grown-up horse with a real grown-up purpose. It meant that I could have a job and make my humans proud.

"I think he is old enough to feel the weight on his back," Kris said.

"I agree," Elaine replied.

The time had come. I was my own horse and my purpose was revealing itself.

Chapter Nine
Moonwalker

The old, bay horse has gray hairs on his face and his eyes are turning a silvery-blue, transformed by wisdom. He has seen much: 4-H fairs, helping kids win their first blue ribbon at a horse show, leaping fences and feeling the wind sweep over his ears, kind words and sweet carrots. His name is Moonwalker.

One day many years ago, he had hurt his leg and that meant he could no longer be ridden. Months passed and he grew older and weaker.

Just the day before this one, he was led into an old, rusty farm truck and driven away from all he knew: his barn, his friends, his humans. He had dutifully loaded without an issue, like he had always done.

Now, he is here in this filthy place where terrified whinnies and rough human voices fill the air. The sound is sharp and urgent, and it rings painfully in Moonwalker's ears. There are many other horses here, and they are all so terribly frightened and hungry. They all fear for their lives. Men poke and yell at some of them to get into a big metal truck. All of the horses' panicked eyes are rimmed with white.

Moonwalker knows exactly where they are headed. It is a place where horses go for the final time. It is the ultimate betrayal.

Moonwalker spots a pretty bay mare with a big pregnant belly in the pen next to his. She has a look of peace on her face, her brow is unworried and her eyes are soft.

Moonwalker keeps his eyes on her so he can connect to her energy. His muscles relax ever-so-slightly. He whinnies to her:

Please, dear mare, tell me what this place is? Why are we here?

The bay mare looks over at the old gelding and softly nickers:

It will all be over soon. Try not to be scared.

Moonwalker's relaxation, only momentary in such a terrible place, gives way to distress—his muscles clench and twist, and it feels like he has nothing but blackness in his belly. He lets out a whinny that fills the air with an urgent cry for help. Kindness. Home.

The bay mare's belly moves and Moonwalker can see the outline of her foal's body undulating from within her. Her foal is very close to being born. How did she end up here, he worries. She looks young and healthy, and she is carrying a foal. She should be grazing in a lush field full of clover, not here.

Moonwalker whinnies again, and again the foal moves in the mare's belly. The foal can hear Moonwalker's cries and is reacting to his pain.

My kind mare, I am so sorry to disturb you and your baby, he apologizes.

Please, don't apologize. We are all scared, the bay mare says.

I don't know why I am here, Moonwalker frets. His fear has caused white, foamy sweat to erupt on his chest and neck.

What is your name? the mare aks.

Moonwalker, he replies, allowing himself to be calmer. Her question was a welcome distraction.

What is yours? he asks.

Emma, says the mare.

Emma, I want us to go home, Moonwalker cries. Where are my friends?

With that, a tall, thin man with yellow hair emerges from the dusty air and approaches Moonwalker with a bright blue halter and gently places it on the gelding's face. The gelding immediately lowers his great head in gratitude as the man pats his neck and rubs his ears. Moonwalker feels a familiar energy emanating from the kind man with blue halter.

"Moonwalker," says the man. "How did you get here? I am so glad I found you. I searched and searched. . . ." His voice trails off as he starts to silently weep.

"Oh, look at you. Let's get you out of here," the man says to the old horse, his tears rolling freely down his face. He snaps a lead rope to Moonwalker's new halter and opens the gate to his pen. Moonwalker strides stiffly and slowly out of the pen and follows this nice man. The gate slams shut with a loud clang behind them. Moonwalker will never hear that gate again.

"You don't belong here. You don't deserve this," the man says over and over. His voice contains anger for the people who betrayed Moonwalker.

Moonwalker suddenly remembers who this man is: He is the gentle blond boy who rode him in shows a long, long time ago. Moonwalker proudly carried this boy, now a man, in front of the judges. Their partnership produced many blue ribbons and proud moments.

Moonwalker remembers all of it—the heat of the summer, the squeak of saddle leather, the dusty show ring, the brightly painted fences, the neck pats and treats for a job well done, the cool baths from the garden hose, the laughter of happy humans. Life was good back then. Moonwalker wonders if he had been a bad horse to be at such a scary place. What had he done wrong? He had tried so hard to be good. He never bit anyone, but once he stepped on a human's foot by mistake and the human yelped in pain. Is that the reason he had been brought here?

Moonwalker knows in his heart that he is a good horse and that this man was here to take him away from the horrible place. Moonwalker also knows that none of the horses left behind are bad horses.

As the man leads him away, Moonwalker knows he is safe. He takes one last look behind him to see Emma peering over the tall rails of the pen. She whinnies to him:

You are safe, Moonwalker!

At the blond man's home there is a big house and a cozy red barn. Inside the big house is a closet. Inside the closet there is a wooden chest. Inside that wooden chest are the blue ribbons and trophies that Moonwalker won with him.

After the man puts Moonwalker in his new stall in the cozy red barn, the man strings the blue ribbons on baling twine and hangs them on the old gelding's door. The ribbons ruffle slightly at the breeze blowing through the barn as if they had come back to life after the many years of hiding in the wooden chest.

The man smiles as the blue ribbons wave in the wind—he remembers when he was small and a big horse named Moonwalker taught him how not to be scared.

The blue ribbons invite all who pass by Moonwalker's stall to marvel at the prize-winning gelding contained within.

He is forever Moonwalker, a good horse who made dreams come true. He is home.

Chapter Ten
The Saddle

The first time I wore a saddle was not a scary experience, even when the girth was pulled tight around my chest. At first it alarmed me—it evoked ancient memories of a predator attempting to take me down. All horses have this memory, even if we have never been in that kind of danger—it is an instinct born to the Family of Horses. But, then I remembered there was no predator—only Kris speaking softly to me and telling me I was a good boy. There was nothing to fear. My eyes softened and I lowered my head into Kris's arms. She stroked my muzzle and a sugar cube appeared in her hand. I gently took her offering and let it surround my tongue with its affirming sweetness.

The saddle felt heavy and unbalanced, but I didn't feel afraid even as it shifted and moved on my beck, because Kris would never ask me to do something scary. The trust I felt for Kris was steady and sure—her consistent and gentle actions never once betrayed me. She honored my true nature by allowing me to explore, to feel, and even to be a little fearful of something new. She gave me time to learn that I was safe and never made feel bad for making a mistake for it meant I was learning. When I did something right, she rewarded me with sugar cubes and gentle words in her rainfall voice.

I wanted to make Kris proud of me. I wanted to carry her on my back and help her to fly. My legs were strong and I was ready, but Kris took her time with me so that my experience was a positive one. Saddle and bridle time was a happy time; unhurried and calm. It was my time with my favorite human. And she always had treats.

Now, let me tell you about the bit and bridle. My leather bridle was like a halter, only heavier—and the bit was a soft rubbery plastic that tasted like an apple. The first time I held it in my mouth, I thought that this thing wasn't bad at all. Kris laughed at me when I rolled the bit in my mouth in an attempt to suck out its sweet apple flavor. My mouth foamed so much it

started to drip and I made loud smacking noises with my lips.

"My goodness, Starry," Kris giggled. "I guess you really like that!"

If this is what it meant to be a grown-up horse, then I was all in. This was delightful! I often shared my training stories with Nala, who always listened with her ears forward and her eyes bright.

...And then Kris walked me around with the saddle on my back and I wanted to carry her, too—but she said I needed to get used the saddle first, I told her.

My first time with a saddle was also my first time with someone on my back, Nala replied. *This human just leapt on my back and started kicking me. I was so frightened!*

What did you do, Nala? I would have been so scared! I asked.

I tried to run away from them, but a big human grabbed the reins and yelled at me to 'whoa', Nala replied. *It was awful. I hated it. I hated the humans who pushed me around. The way Kris is training you is the right way to do it. She honors our Family.*

Why do some humans act in such a harsh way? I asked her.

Some humans are unkind, because the world was unkind to them, Nala said simply. *It is a horse's greatest misfortune to be in the care of a cruel human.*

Can cruel humans ever learn to be kind? I continued.

Yes, Nala said, her voice heavy with wisdom. *They can learn. And, horses can help teach them.*

We can do that? I wondered.

Yes, we can, Stardust, Nala answered. *Horses are among the Ancient Beings. We hold more wisdom than the sky above us. It was my mother who taught me that. My mother was the wisest horse I have ever known.*

You have a mommy, Nala? I said, my eyes widening with curiosity. *Where is she?*

Be silent now, my young friend, Nala replied as her energy dimmed and grew pale. Her eyes became worried and wide. I thought she might weep.

I suddenly felt terrible for making Nala forlorn—I didn't mean to hurt her with my innocent question. How could I have been so careless? Ah yes, sometimes we say things that don't mean to hurt—but they do. I learned from my mommy that when we say or do something by mistake that causes another being pain, we were to apologize without hesitation—then take steps to never do or say that hurtful thing ever again.

My apology to Nala was swift and heartfelt:

I am sorry Nala. I want you to know that if you ever want to talk about your mommy, I would love to listen. I am sure she was a splendid horse with a breathtaking beauty.

At that moment, Nala's energy brightened again as she said to me:

Thank you, Stardust. Talking about her makes me feel like she is still right beside me. I will share her with you.

Nala's eyes drifted to the sky and followed some passing clouds for a few moments, then she spoke:

My mother was the finest horse with the most generous heart, Nala said. *She now lives in the clouds above us. She is up there, Stardust, and she is smiling for me right now. I was her last baby. She cared for me and loved me with all of her being. She protected me.*

Thank you, Nala, I said. *Any time you want to remember her, please know I am here for you. I want to know more about the mare who raised you.*

Nala offered me her radiant smile energy, and her eyes lifted and followed the clouds once more before lowering her head to graze on the clover at her feet. The unhurried and beautiful energy surrounding her was a soft rose pink—and it let me know that Nala's mother was all around her, still protecting her baby.

She is always up there, never far away from me, was all Nala said.

The rose-pink energy that encircled her sparkled with such a brilliant and blinding force that it almost hurt to gaze upon it. Bits of broken golden stars twinkled in the energy's outer circle—danced, twirled, flew—and vanished. They told me that a mother's love is strong and ever-present.

The broken golden stars carried their message of undying love to the galaxies and beyond. I kept a few of the pieces in my heart for safekeeping.

Chapter Eleven
At Night, There Are Many Stars

One night, when the sky was an infinite black and the stars winked and glimmered, I had another dream. As I drifted to sleep, the moon rose, sweeping light over the blue-black sky and flooding my stall with its pale silvery glow.

I was in my pond in my mommy's tummy again, and I could hear the high-pitched whinny of one particular horse. This horse spoke to my mommy.

This horse's voice was raspy like he had been whinnying in terror all day. I trembled and twitched in my watery home as I heard his cries and felt his pain. This horse was trying very hard to be brave. He had many unanswered questions.

Then, I heard the voice of my mommy—muffled and watery: *It will all be over soon. Try not to be scared.*

Then, I heard the horse's name: *Moonwalker.*

Then, the image of a little red barn bathed in yellow summer sunlight.

Then, the image of wide, open fields filled with emerald-green grass, cheerful dandelions, and playful dragonflies.

Then, the image of a big, old bay gelding with unworried, cloudy eyes and gray hairs flecking his gentle face.

When I awoke, I discovered that the moonlight flooded my stall and was fully embracing me in what I can only describe as home. I felt it lift my heart skyward with its silvery glow.

It was then that I knew that Moonwalker was home, too.

I had met him before I was born.

Moonwalker, I said softly into the night air. *Welcome home, old friend.*

Chapter Twelve
When Legs Are Tired, Hearts Are Strong

It is auction day, and the big mare moves hesitantly as a harsh hand from a faceless human roughly smacks her hind end and yells gruffly at her.

"Get moving!" the man demands impatiently.

Ah, she wants to be cooperative and do as the angry man orders, but her left hind leg holds in it an immense pain that shoots right down to her massive hoof; burning and sharp like hot embers shooting off of a farrier's anvil.

Please, I can't move so quickly, the big mare pleads to the man with her large, liquid eyes.

Just then, another horse bumps the man out of the way to stand next to her. The big mare's heart gladdens with gratitude at the kind gesture.

The man walks away in defeat and starts smacking the other horses in the pen. He needs to move them out to the auction area so they can get out of here—by rescue or otherwise. He shouts with urgency and anger, and the horses fear him. Some take aim at him with their legs and teeth.

They know that this place is not home. They know they are not safe.

The big mare, resplendent in her golden coat and creamy flaxen mane and tail, is able to rest for a spell, thanks to her new friend—a pregnant bay mare.

My name is Emma, the pregnant bay mare says. I will stay right here beside you. Please lean on me if you must, I see that your leg is swollen and your hoof is infected. Please rest.

My humans called me Daisy Mae, the big mare says with tears forming in her

eyes. I don't know where they are.

Emma simply smiles at Daisy Mae, sending to her heart a bounty of calm and peace in the middle of the chaos.

Please, just lean on me, I am strong, Emma offers.

But I see that you pregnant, Daisy Mae frets. I am a big Belgian draft horse; I am far too heavy for you to hold up.

I have you, rest your leg, Emma says.

Daisy Mae leans gently into Emma's neck and chest, and Emma holds firm. Daisy Mae lets out a long, whuffling breath of relief. The great mare lowers her tired head.

Emma and Daisy Mae rest on each other for quite some time—Daisy Mae falls asleep. She is so, so tired. So hungry. Emma does not falter and stands for both of them.

Then, Daisy Mae sees the trailer. Then, she feels the nylon halter slipping onto her face.

Is this the end? Is this it? She worries. I can no longer pull a cart or carry a rider. I have no purpose and no one wants me.

Then the soft words from a gentle human fill her ears:

"Come this way, big girl, go slow, we are getting you out of here."

Oh joy, oh bliss! Kindness has arrived!

Daisy Mae responds to the kindness and wills her painful hind leg with the infected hoof to move her forward. One step, two steps…the pain sears her leg bones right to the marrow. She knows she must keep walking even if her leg does not want to.

"Good girl, come with me, you are safe," says the human at the end of the lead rope.

As Daisy Mae hobbles forward, Emma gently steps back to allow the big mare to walk to safety. When Daisy Mae no longer feels Emma's comfort, she panics.

Wait, wait! Daisy Mae wails. My friend Emma has a foal inside of her, take her too! Please! Don't leave her!

"Come on, beautiful," the human urges with a soft voice. "You're okay. I wish I could take all of your friends home with me. I really do."

But my friend, Daisy Mae whinnies with fright and panic. My friend!

As Daisy Mae walks onto the trailer, she tugs on the lead rope to take one last look behind her. She sees Emma looking over the metal rail with her ears perked, calm and peaceful amongst the other panicked horses in the pens. Emma looks straight at Daisy Mae and calls out to her:

Go, be safe, be loved, Daisy Mae!

Find your way home, Emma! Thank you for your kindness! Daisy Mae responds with a shrill, fluttering neigh that holds a magnificent power that could pierce a soul. Find your way home, promise me!

I promise, Emma says.

The human latches the trailer gate and Daisy Mae greets another horse in the trailer. The kind humans saved her, too. Her eyes are sunken and her ribs are showing through her red patchwork coat. She nickers a sweet welcome to the big mare.

Where are we going? Daisy Mae asks her.

We are going to a safe place where gentle humans are waiting for us. There are friends. And food. And big paddocks under a beaming blue sky, she answers.

She is a small red mare with the biggest, saddest eyes Daisy Mae has ever seen.

My leg hurts, will they help me? Daisy Mae continues.

Yes, the small red mare answers. We will all have help. You are safe now, quiet your mind.

The trailer moves slowly and Daisy Mae steadies herself, careful not to put weight on her bad leg. There is a full hay net right at her nose. She reaches out and takes a mouthful. It is fragrant and green and she can't eat it fast enough. It fills her empty, groaning belly with its golden-green bounty. The small red mare eats her hay as well, and the two new friends enjoy their banquet as the trailer travels the busy highway to their new home.

Many hours later, Daisy Mae and the small red mare arrive at a place called a "sanctuary." It is a place that wraps its strong and safe arms around them, promis-

ing never to let go. It is a place where hunger and fear are unwelcome.

As Daisy Mae is led into the barn, a stall full of golden straw and downy sawdust await her. A vet will visit her tomorrow morning to treat her infected hoof—but for now, the kind people at the sanctuary wrap her hoof in soft cotton bandages infused with a soothing salve. The pain subsides the moment the salve coats her hoof and Daisy Mae lets out a grateful sigh, emptying her big lungs and allowing her shoulders to drop. The big mare can finally rest. The humans tending to her stroke her tired face and softly pat her neck. Their voices are kind and their hands are gentle.

Daisy Mae, the big golden mare, is home and the fear leaves her eyes forever.

Chapter Thirteen
When the Purpose Becomes Clear

The first day Kris sat on my back was a day that will forever live in my heart as one of my most proud moments.

Kris sat tall in the saddle, and I felt her weight on my back and her unshakable energy coursed through me like a river. I wanted to move forward with her and create beauty like she did with Tara and Nala. I had waited so long for this moment—and now that it was here, I desired to make my purpose clear. I was a rescued colt who had grown to be the Gentleman of Faraway. I had a reason to be here, right now, in this moment. My legs felt as if they contained wings. Let's go!

"Good boy, Buddy," Kris said as she patted my neck. "This is no big deal, right?"

She often called me Buddy, and I loved the name. It meant I was her friend. We were in this together.

Elaine, watching from her chair in the corner of the arena, quietly cheered us on:

"He looks spectacular. What a grand horse he is," she observed.

I felt as if I would burst open like a seedpod in the first rain of spring. I was a grown horse. I was pure power and energy. I was proud of who I had become.

Kris gently squeezed my sides, and I instinctively walked forward. That's what Nala told me to do. I was a good student and wanted to get everything right on the first day—so I had studied ahead of time.

"Nice walk there, Buddy," Kris cooed at me. "You glide and stretch like a champ. Good boy."

"Oh my, he's a dressage horse," Elaine said from her corner. "Just those few strides and I can tell."

Kris felt light and balanced on my back—I wanted to do more than walk. I wanted to trot out all fancy and high-stepping like Tara. I walked with newfound purpose and allowed my limbs to cover the ground in an effortless stride to show Kris I was ready. My back was loose and swinging and Kris followed my movement; her legs lightly touching my sides.

"We are just going to walk today, Buddy," Kris answered me as she squeezed the reins. I felt the rubbery apple-flavored bit pull back slightly on my lips and I knew that this meant to slow down. So I did. Nala had told me that, too.

"Does this horse know everything already?" Elaine marveled. "He isn't fussing or anything. It's like he has done this a million times before!"

I smiled to myself and heard Nala's patient instruction circling in my mind:

Move forward when she squeezes with her legs, go slower when you feel the bit pulling you, and don't be silly and throw your head up or anything. Kris will tell you exactly what to do. She is a very considerate rider. Just have fun.

My first ride was now out of the way. Bring on the fancy stuff!

Chapter Fourteen
Bring Me Home

That night, I had a dream about a big mare with a gleaming golden coat and an ivory mane and tail. She galloped effortlessly over an open field comprised of great pillowy clouds, whinnying and flying free. Her creamy mane and tail ebbed like an ocean wave with each bounding stride; the joy contained within her was now free and unfettered. Her large, otherworldly eyes sparkled and reflected many years of love and friends. She whinnied her delight to me—and even in my dream, I felt myself galloping right alongside her.

Your mother saved me, I am so happy both of you found your way home! The mare whinnied in a sweet, singsong voice that glowed with pink stars as it wended its way around the clouds.

I found my way home, too—and now I live in the clouds. I knew love and safety in my life and at the end my nice lady fed me sugar cubes, she continued, a heavenly wind unfurling her mane like a flag.

Who are you? I asked the big mare.

Daisy Mae! She answered as she lifted her head high and whuffled playfully through her nostrils.

My mother saved you? I asked her as I galloped alongside her. It was hard to keep up—she was as swift as a starling.

Yes! Oh yes, she did! May your mother be blessed with love for the rest of her days. When she arrives at the clouds a long, long time from this moment, I will gallop up to her and share my gratitude with her, Daisy Mae whinnied joyfully.

Then, with a snort and a buck, she disappeared into a powder-blue cloud. I watched her until the last wisp of her graceful tail was no longer visible.

The beautiful golden mare named Daisy Mae. My mommy had saved her.

My mommy had also saved me.

When I awakened, the barn was dark except for a faint sliver of moonlight peering through the window of my stall. I lifted my head and followed it—and what I saw was a gathering of silver-violet clouds cavorting and dancing around the moon, celebrating its light. The air held a silent, cool breeze—and I thought I heard the clouds singing to me:

Daisy Mae! Daisy Mae! Daisy Mae!

Chapter Fifteen
Purpose Lifts the Heart

Kris rode me several times a week, always making sure she didn't push me too quickly. Her patient ways allowed me to see my purpose with great clarity—with each new task she taught me, I saw my future filled with proud moments carrying Kris in a dressage arena. Kris was my best friend and I was ever grateful that she chose me as her horse. I wanted to do right by her and be the best partner I could be.

I still saw my mommy when I was turned out in my paddock after my rides. She was still as beautiful as ever; her fiery bay coat glowing in the rays of the sun. When I started having my dreams, I discovered that my mommy was much, much more than just a pretty mare with big eyes. She had a noble purpose. A purpose so grand in its scope and profound in its truth, that it allowed her to save lives.

Moonwalker and Daisy Mae knew this.

I knew this.

My mommy's purpose was bequeathed to her by the sky and the Universe—she had been sent to the Bad Place to soothe the hearts of the scared horses who were panicked to the point of near collapse. She went to these horses, stood right next to them and told them to lean on her when they felt weak. For the horses who went for a final ride on the Bad Truck, she told them it would be over soon and the pain would be gone. She assured them that the clouds would forever hold them in a gossamer embrace. She let them know that there was no pain in the clouds.

My mommy's voice was soft and kind—always so kind. These thin, scared horses felt their hearts lift a little at the thought of a willowy, heavenly place where unimaginable hurt and fear would never touch them again.

For the ones rescued and given more time on the earthly plane, she always whinnied at them her elation.

The rescued horses had new halters slipped over their heads, letting them know that the bighearted human at the other end of that taut lead rope would never let go.

Am I really going to be okay? These horses wondered at that moment.

Then, my mommy's joyful whinny calling after them told them all they needed to know:

You are safe! Be loved!

And the fear….

….disappeared.

I have heard of horses who perform what humans call miracles—events that cannot be explained by logic or mathematical equations. Miracles were performed by a being otherworldly—a being devoted to listening to the heart and the soul and allowing energy to flow through the channels of Beyond. It was then that the magic within could be allowed to dance and swirl. It was then that Purpose became clear.

Every so often, this being from Beyond walked amongst us to offer peace and calm to our troubled hearts. Sometimes this being arrived in the form of a horse.

That was my mommy. The horses she comforted called her Emma.

As I saw her contentedly grazing on the grass that cradled her hooves, I thought how lucky I was to have such a mommy. She was mine, and I was hers. Her divine and humble blood flowed through my veins.

Because of this, I felt that my purpose stretched beyond the dressage arena, and I was eager to experience its breadth.

Chapter Sixteen
Fire Fed by the Bellows

My training sessions with Kris were filled with fun and learning. Kris was a skilled rider, yes, but she also knew my language. When I was nervous, she would reach down and touch my neck with her fingers and tell me everything was okay. Her words and touch told me that it was okay to be unsure, and that she was always there to help. I was never punished or pushed. I was never scolded or smacked. Kris was gentle—but firm. There was never a question as to what she required of me and I was a quick learner. She provided me with the structure and leadership a young horse in training needed. I felt safe.

Our trot work started to shine and with Kris's gentle cues, I learned to extend my legs and cover the ground with powerful strides. The day she asked me for my first canter with her on my back was a day I will never forget: I was a proud and elegant horse arching my neck and engaging my powerful hindquarters to propel myself into a rolling three-beat gait. Kris sat perfectly aligned with my spine and followed my movement; ebbing and flowing like the tide.

I felt something new grow within me that day—it was a fire deep within my chest and it burned brightly. The fire glowed with such force and strength that it loosened a tight knot in my being. No more youthful nervousness existed at that moment.

With my breath, I released the remaining tension in my muscles and just allowed myself to soar…

…And then…

I was free as an owl in silent flight; swooping over open fields with playful abandon. The arena felt light and springy beneath my hooves. I was pow-

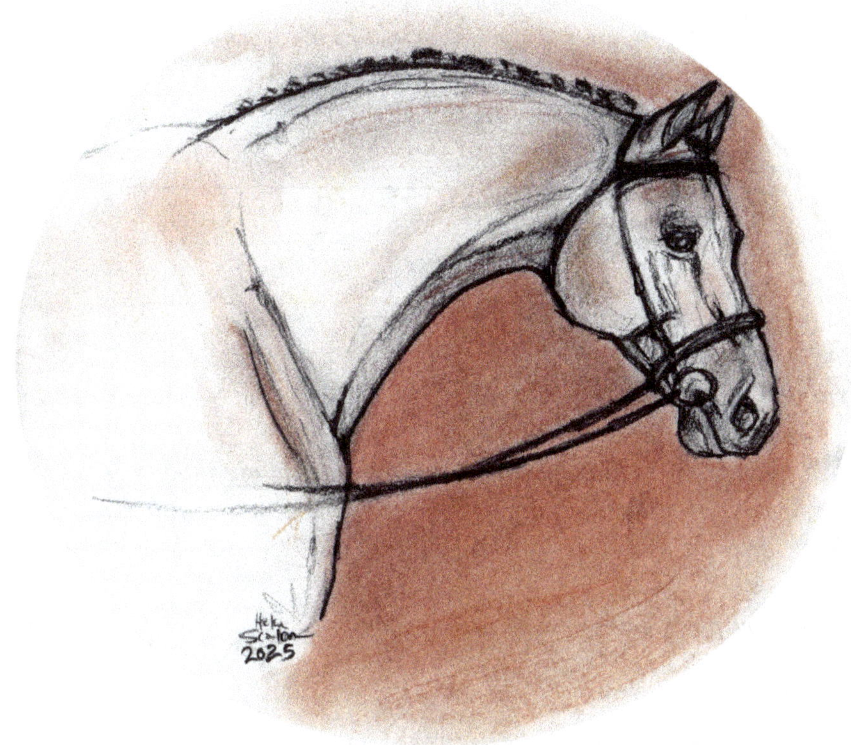

ered by instinct, my foal days long behind me. I could now keep up with Daisy Mae in my dream. My nostrils grew wide and glowed red from the energy coursing through me. With each blowing breath, straining sinew, and resounding beat of my heart, I was a bellows feeding the fire within me.

It was the day that changed everything.

I was horse who garnered tears of awe and hushed whispers of admiration.

I was a horse who made dreams real.

I was a horse who made flight possible.

I was a horse who inspired artists and poets.

I was a horse worthy of carrying angels.

I was a dressage horse.

Chapter Seventeen
The Dark Gelding

I am so angry, the dark gelding's energy screams.

Leave me alone.

The dark gelding bares his big, yellow teeth and threatens to use them on the young woman with the grain bucket. The young woman stands firm. Calmly and confidently, tells the gelding to back up.

Okay, you have a big voice and you aren't scared of me, says the dark gelding with his eyes. I will back up.

As soon as he moves away from the young woman, she drops the grain in his empty bucket, and leaves the stall. She slides his stall door shut and latches it.

The dark gelding is still at the back of the stall, ears laced back and eye whites flashing.

"You can eat, it's okay," says the young woman.

Her voice is steady and soft like a forest stream.

The dark gelding does not move. His four hooves stay firm on the straw bedding in his stall.

I don't trust you, his energy says to her. You will hurt me and send me away—back to the Bad Place. I won't go near you. You will take me back there. You may have a soft voice, but you have two legs. Two-legged creatures have hurt me and betrayed me.

"It's okay," the young woman says again. "Look, I will leave now so you can eat in

peace. I will see you tomorrow morning."

As the young woman leaves the barn, the dark gelding buries his face in his bucket and devours the molasses-coated oats. He furiously crushes the plump hulls with his molars thinking that it may be the last time he eats for a long while.

The Bad Place didn't have oats or water.

The Bad Place held only pain and fear.

The dark gelding knows that this is a cruel trick like the last time he was fed a proper meal. It was then that the truck took him away.

I am not falling for that again, the dark gelding says to himself as he chews another mouthful of oats. They said they loved me. They didn't love me. No one loves me now. I will not be fooled.

The young woman arrives the next morning with another bucket of oats. She tops off his water bucket and gives him all the hay he can eat. This time, she doesn't leave. She stays until the dark gelding feels safe to emerge from the corner of his stall and eat his breakfast.

The young woman stands as still as she can. A soft breeze blows through the barn to slightly tousle her hair. The dark gelding eats and eats and eats as she stands there. He can hear her heart beating. He can hear her breath.

She does not move, at all.

She arrives again that evening to feed him again. Then again the next morning. Then the next day. And the next. And the next.

On this day, the sky is bright without a cloud. The air is warm with spring. The young woman reaches to touch the dark gelding's face as he eats his hay.

The dark gelding allows the young woman's fingers to gently sweep over his muzzle.

Nothing about her energy feels like the Bad Place.

The young woman then reaches to scratch the dark gelding's ears. He blissfully leans into her touch as her fingers itch the inflamed fly bites that gouged his tender skin when he was at the Bad Place. Finally, relief.

Then, the halter gently slips over his head. She doesn't impatiently pull on the lead rope. She gives him space.

He follows her—one hoof tentatively following the next. The young woman lets him take his time.

When they approach his paddock, she swings the gate open and unclips the lead rope from his halter. The dark gelding doesn't walk away. He stays near the young woman because she feels safe. He trusts her.

"Go ahead and play," the young woman says joyfully.

Can I? he asks her. Will you come back?

"I will be right here, every day," her energy answers.

And she is true to her word.

She comes back. Every day.

The dark gelding, now named Windborne, knows that his anger was fear. And now that fear is crushed—just like the oats he devoured. The Bad Place recedes into his memory and fades as newsprint does when it is exposed to the sun.

Love makes that happen.

Windborne has love.

He never bares his teeth again.

Chapter Eighteen
Windborne

I had a dream one night that I met a handsome dark gelding who looked a lot like me. His coat was the color of polished mahogany, and his eyes were almost a pure, glassy black. They shone with such nobility and strength that my breath caught in my throat—even in my dream. He was simply spectacular.

The dream saw us trotting together in perfect harmony, matching each step with power and grace. We were in a magnificent riding arena filled with light and many people watching. They cheered and clapped for us.

I could sense from this dark gelding that he had seen many terrible things and had experienced great cruelty—but his now heart only contained joy. Joy for being alive. Joy for his health. Joy for his elegance. Joy for his friends, both human and horse. Joy for making people happy watching his floating trot.

It seemed as if his hooves never touched the ground; he was a weightless being capable of effortless flight.

The dark gelding and I trotted for what seemed an eternity—and we never tired. We could just trot and trot and feel that joy forever.

Before the dream ended, the dark gelding turned to me and tossed his grand head in the air making his wavy forelock whip up like the wings of a heron. His black eyes met mine and he said to me:

I am Windborne. You will know me.

To feel such freedom, such happiness for being alive, to see such elegance, to know how it felt to demand the attention of admiring humans—it was as if this was more than a dream. It was as if it really happened.

Did a dark gelding named Windborne just visit me?

Would I know him?

Chapter Nineteen
The Show

The time had finally arrived! I was to perform in my first dressage competition with Kris on my back.

I knew how to get on the horse trailer because I had done it when I was a foal, and Kris had practiced loading me long before show day. The trailer was no longer a scary thing, now it held the promise of a fun and exciting day.

And, Nala was coming with me!

We rode side-by-side in the trailer as we helped ourselves to our full hay nets. Trees, road signs, and cars passed us by as Kris drove us to our destination: the Enchanted Acres dressage schooling show. It was a favorite of many riders; they waited all year to perform their tests in front of the judge and showcase how hard they worked to form a harmonious partnership with their horses.

The show grounds were practically buzzing with action—horses being unloaded from their trailers, riders nervously studying their tests, tacking up, last-minute polish for both human and horse—and of course, the dressage arena. There were so many beautiful horses gleaming with health and energy trotting, cantering, doing shoulder-ins and leg yields for the judge in his booth—a kind-looking man in a perfectly white shirt. Apparently, this judge was quite accomplished as a rider and a trainer, and his many accomplishments in the dressage arena made him a popular and respected judge. He was, as Kris said, a "big deal." He gave off a congenial and warm energy that immediately put me at ease.

In the booth sitting next next to the judge was the dutiful scribe. Her responsibility was to document everything the judge said about the horse's movements and the rider's ability—"nice use of the corner" "circle cut off" "nice straight centerline," etc. She clearly enjoyed her job. She smiled at every horse and rider in the arena, instantly earing nervousness and tension. Seeing friendly faces in the judge's booth helped the riders to relax and have fun. In turn, their horses could relax as well.

I tried to relax, but I could not wait to get in that arena and make that "big deal" judge give me high marks. I wanted Kris to be proud of me.

Kris rode Nala first, and as they trotted their circles and cantered down the long diagonal, I saw my purpose become crystal. A dressage show was a celebration of the partnership between human and horse; a partnership forged through history and created with an unbreakable bond. The horse is to love his or her work—no impatient tail swishing, jaw clenching, or scared eyes. This can only happen when the rider and horse are speaking the same language. There is no force, no pushing, no pulling. Just smooth, flowing gaits that cover the ground in an effortless dance.

This takes many, many hours of training for both horse and rider—and you would never know it because the dressage horse and rider make look easy. But, my dear readers, it is not.

Just as it takes time for a young human to learn language, it also takes time to create the happy partnership in the dressage arena. There is much to know—balance, bending, rhythm, , straightness, impulsion, and halting with all four feet perfectly square. The rider gives the horse cues and direction through his or her hands, legs, seat, and weight. All of these elements of the joyous horse and rider dance must work together in order for our movements to look beautiful.

The rider must sit tall, deep, and straight with still hands—even when we are cantering and powerfully bounding over what seems like acres with each stride. It takes many hours of patient instruction for a rider to achieve this competency in the saddle.

And, when it all comes together—the horse and rider dance is the very definition of harmony, rhythm, and balance.

I was able to watch Nala and Kris perform their test from a safe distance because Elaine led me out of the trailer so I could graze and become familiar with my new surroundings. I wasn't scared, I was excited!

Nala looked regal in her shimmering platinum coat and her hooves polished with black oil. Kris wore a black jacket, white gloves, white breeches, and tall black boots I had never seen before. They were her special show boots, reserved for when she needed to look her best.

My ears perked up and my keen eyesight allowed me to take in the whole scene. They rode their test perfectly. Nala performed all of her movements with grace and willingness; Kris's cues were imperceptible. They truly moved as one.

When Nala trotted down the arena's centerline and halted in a perfect square, Kris saluted the judge. It was then that the applause rose up like tidal wave. Nala and Kris gave the audience a lovely picture of trust and teamwork between rider and horse. Many knew Nala's story of how Kris rescued her, ribby and dirty, from a muddy backyard and it made their accomplishments in the dressage arena that much more remarkable. It was a display of Nala's resilience and Kris's unwavering care—the result was a friendship based on trust that translated into brilliance in the equestrian arts.

At that shining moment, I realized that I was rescued by Kris, too—and I wanted to give her that applause. I wanted to thank her for giving me and my mommy a home. I wanted to thank her for giving me a purpose. I wanted to thank her for her belief in me. I wanted to thank her for being patient with me and allowing me to learn. I wanted to thank her for allowing me to become my own horse. I was the Gentleman of Faraway—I wanted to prove that, today. In that arena.

I was ready.

As I watched Nala and Kris exit the arena, people still clapping, I started snorting impatiently, my eyes wide and rimmed with white.

"Steady there, kid," Elaine laughed. I pawed at the ground in an attempt to speed up time. "You will get in there and strut your stuff soon enough!"

Then, it was our turn. Kris took the reins from Elaine and gave my neck a quick touch with her gloved hand. It felt warm and reassuring. She handed Nala to Elaine, removed the saddle from her back, and put it on mine. Kris tightened the girth and double checked all of my tack to be sure everything was set to go.

As Kris gently landed in the saddle on my back, she cooed at me, "my handsome boy, you just have fun and remember what I taught you."

She softly touched my neck again, and I tugged at the bit in my mouth to let her know I was ready to get in that arena and dance with her. I breathed in my excitement and I puffed out my chest. As I bowed my neck and stomped the earth under my hooves, Kris had to struggle a little to keep the reins steady. Kris laughed as I started prancing in place in anticipation. I could feel Kris's energy through her boots—she was as eager as I was.

Let's do this! I told her.

Then, her legs squeezed my sides and I knew that was my cue to trot. I channeled my excitement into beautiful and correct dressage movements: Floating, forward, my neck arched, we waited for the bell from the judge's booth. When the bell sounded, it meant we could enter the dressage arena and perform our test.

The bell finally rang out with a bright metallic clang, and we found our way down the centerline. My first dressage test was about to begin.

I trotted with confidence and power, and as Kris closed her hands on the reins and sat deep in the saddle, I halted squarely and in perfect balance. Kris dropped her right hand and quickly nodded her head in a salute to the judge. She gathered the reins and off we went into a working trot. Our circles were round and correct. I was perfectly obedient for my transition from trot to canter—and I got the right lead. Kris rode me deeply into the corner to set me up for a more ground-covering trot on the diagonal line through the arena. Suddenly, I was racing with Daisy Mae in my dreams. I was the barred owl in silent flight. I was the minnow in a stream.

I was the dressage horse in the arena.

I felt the sun warming my flanks and heard the whispers of "look at him" as I performed my test.

Our final centerline was straight and exactly on the mark—and Kris had barely lifted her head from her final salute when the enthusiastic applause rang out. That applause was for us. Our ride. For me. For Kris.

Kris reached down, let the reins go slack, and threw her arms around my neck in a loving hug. My heart felt as if it could burst from my chest from holding so much joy.

I did it.

"Good boy, Buddy," Kris said as her arms embraced me; her smile as bright as the sun. "Good, good boy!"

Elaine greeted us when we exited the arena, a smile beamed from her face like the millions of stars in the universe.

"This horse has such talent," she said as she patted my neck and held the reins as Kris dismounted. When Kris landed on the ground, she bounced up on her toes with a happy little jump.

"That's my boy!" she exclaimed. "He is the Gentleman of Faraway."

I felt that her eyes were wet as she buried her face in my neck. Tears? Was she sad?

"To think you were almost thrown away like garbage," she choked through her tears. "To think…you almost…"

I bent my neck so my muzzle could reach the sleeve of her jacket. I nuzzled the fabric in an attempt to comfort her.

Don't be sad. I am here.

"Good boy, good boy, good boy," was all Kris said in that moment.

She said it over and over. She kept saying it until the words were forever branded on my heart.

It is every horse's dream to be loved this much.

Chapter Twenty
The Blue Ribbon

It was made of a silky, shiny fabric that was clipped to my bridle in a shining moment of pride. It waved like butterfly wings when the breeze picked up.

My first show, my first time in the show arena….

My scores were high enough to win that blue ribbon.

Nala won one, too.

Be proud of what you have accomplished, Nala said to me when we were side-by-side on the trailer on our way home. *You worked hard and learned much. You earned it.*

Thank you, Nala—I learned so much from you. I could not have done this without your friendship, I told her.

What she said next fell on my ears with such a resounding sweetness—the words seemed to glimmer like rays of the sun on a pond:

I am proud of you, Stardust.

These words came from a mare who used to live in a paddock with mud up to her knees. A mare who had given up hope of finding joy and purpose. A mare who had forgotten the taste of a sugar cube and the sparkling brightness of clean water to drink. A mare who had been thrown away and deemed too dangerous, too unpredictable, too unmanageable.

A mare who had overcome fear and learned to trust. A mare who gave her whole heart to the kindness of her trustworthy friends, horse and human.

A mare who was a brilliant, silver-tailed comet in the dressage arena…

…She was proud of *me*.

Chapter Twenty One
The Stars

Kris took me to many shows that summer—and I began to draw a crowd of adoring humans who loved watching me perform my tests. I won many classes with high scores—and it seemed that Kris and I were unstoppable. I just wanted to show her my gratitude for giving me a safe home and an education that was forged in patience and kindness.

Kris gave me something that all horses long for: a purpose. Kris called me her "honors student" and showed me how to perform some of the more advanced moves like the shoulder-in and half-pass. I relished our training sessions and could not wait to show Kris that I could handle anything she asked of me. Her instruction allowed me the space and time to figure it all out—and when I "nailed it" Kris could not contain her elation and pride. It was then that I got the neck pats and her high-pitched, singsong praise of "good job, Buddy!" The time we spent at the shows was the culmination of the hard work and discipline—our investment in each other and our friendship was evident to all of the judges and spectators.

Kris and I attracted a bit of a following because of our success at the shows—so many people wanted to see the rescue horse with the star on his forehead perform a brilliant and near-perfect dressage test. I became famous for my canter: it was correct and balanced, but also animated and beautiful to watch. Whenever Kris slipped her leg back behind the girth to ask me to canter I brought my hind legs under me and lifted off the ground like a raptor in flight. When I extended my stride, I could hear the gasps of awe from the sidelines: *what a gorgeous animal, so elegant, so strong, so brilliant…*

With my heart and my lungs pumping like bellows, I celebrated my strength. All the while, I felt Kris' smile energy holding my spirit in a radiant embrace.

"That horse and his mother were rescued from the auction—she was pregnant with him," I heard a human say as I passed by on my way to the arena for my test.

"Yes, they were both on their way to the truck—how absolutely horrible," replied another.

"He is something out of a dream, I can't believe he came so close to not being here," another said.

"I know his dam, she is the sweetest horse I've ever met," another replied. "When she was in her pen at the auction, I heard she let a Belgian with an injured hoof lean on her. Can you imagine? Just this very pregnant little thing, letting a huge draft horse rest on her. Just a beautiful soul."

My mommy! These people knew my mommy! My heart soared.

With every stride in the dressage arena, I thought of her. I thought of me living in the pond in her tummy and how she helped other horses in our scary situation. To live free, moving in harmony with the kind human who rescued me, was everything. It was why I was there. The Bad Place was far, far away.

The high scores and encouraging comments from the judges piled up even more. Those scores meant I was a dressage champion, and the satin ribbons became larger and more colorful. Kris hung them up on my stall for all to see and admire.

Then, one beautiful day Kris gave me some news—we were chosen to do a demonstration at a huge horse event in the next state over. She told me I would ride in the trailer for almost two hours. This must be a big deal because when Kris leaned against my neck to tell me, I felt her heart jump like rabbit from deep within her. I matched her eenergy and nickered excitedly.

"You and I are going to show a big crowd of people how a rescue horse can be a beautiful dressage partner," Kris explained. "You are going to inspire people to rescue their own horses."

Her rainfall voice enfolded me as she stroked my neck and scratched my ears. Then she told me this:

"You will save lives, Buddy. Just by being you."

Just like my mommy!

The demonstration was held in the biggest show arena I had ever seen. It had seats that seemed to reach into the sky—and so many people were there to see me and other rescue horses show off our talents. Lights as bright as the midday sun highlighted the arena.

First, there was a muscular chestnut gelding in a big Western saddle who showed off his barrel racing ability. He and his young rider—a brave girl with black hair tucked under her helmet—deftly twisted around tall, metal barrels to the cheers of an excited crowd. At the end of their demo, the gelding's ears shot straight up because he knew he did a good job. The girl patted his neck and shoulder as her smile lit up the space around them as if they were surrounded by fireflies. The pair excitedly accepted the applause from the adoring crowd as they walked the perimeter of the arena, sweat-soaked and proud.

As Kris and I awaited our turn in the aisle leading into the arena, my mind was abuzz wondering where that brilliant chestnut gelding's life had been like before he was saved. Had he been in the dreaded "number ten" pen my mommy had told me about? The pen that held the "last chance" horses? Had he been discovered covered in mud, forgotten in a backyard, with his ribs protruding?

There was no more time to ponder this as we were called into the arena with several other rescued dressage horses. We trotted out, one by one, to the applause of that wonderfully friendly crowd. I scanned the seats as I trotted by and I saw that nearly every seat in that arena was occupied. Many humans drove many miles to see us on that day.

There were four of us total, trotting with our legs high and our necks arched. The sound of human hands clapping filled the space with a joyous sound that made all of us naturally smile. All of us, riders and horses, beamed our pride under those sun-bright arena lights. We were all triumphant survivors.

Then, Kris's leg slipped back and I knew it was time to for me canter. As I brought my legs under me, moving forward seamlessly, I heard a few whispers from the crowd in my sensitive ears. The energy in those whispers told me:

You are a beautiful horse, something out of a dream...

Kris's fingers were light on the reins, allowing me to unfurl my whole body in a delicate dance built on trust—and even though the crowd was the biggest I had ever seen—I felt no fear. I felt only the moment.

Kris had always been kind to me—even when I was a naughty colt learning my manners. Because of this kindness, I was allowed to flourish without limits.

Kindness led me to my purpose. It led me to this moment in this big arena.

As Kris brought me back to a walk, another dark gelding trotted near us. He was a big horse—taller than me—with powerful, thick legs that covered the ground with confident strides. His hoofbeats vibrated with exquisite might as they struck the ground in a commanding one-two rhythm. His gleaming black eyes resembled polished glass.

I watched him from the corner of my eye and I suddenly felt compelled to reach out to him with my energy, it was as if I had seen him before—but I couldn't remember when or where. I asked him:

I am Stardust, who are you?

He responded with a snort and slight tousle of his refined head:

Windborne.

Windborne?

Windborne....?

Was it truly the horse from my dream? The horse who matched powerful strides with me in the clouds of my slumber? How could this be?

I know you! I replied excitedly.

At that moment, I felt Kris's legs gently squeeze my sides asking me to trot again. I caught up with Windborne and we trotted side-by-side, just like in my dream. How was it that his magnificent horse knew me? How could he have crossed the Universe and all of its stars and galaxies to have met me without me knowing it?

He snorted and answered me:

And I know you. I remember your mother. She comforted me in the Bad Place. I will always remember her kindness to me when I thought all was lost. Yes, I know you....

I felt a chill course through my me, right to my core—it was icy, but not cold. It was a feeling that did not scare me but told me that I had been a small part of something much, much bigger than I. Something that could be described as magic—the force that my first-ever friend was named after. It was something that could not be explained by horse or human, but it most certainly could be felt. The force known as magic told us that we are all a part of the big, big sky above us—and that sky would always lead us home. Home is where we were not only known, but loved.

The not-cold chill was was soon replaced with an all-enveloping warmth that felt like the first rays of the sun that peek over the horizon. A truth sparked in my heart: Windborne met me before I was born. He had reached out to me when I was still in the pond in my mommy's tummy.

Then, I remembered: I had been scared for myself, floating in my pond, and for my mommy, as she tried to be brave and comfort others. Windborne had sent that warmth to me one day as a gesture of love. The Family of Horses was bound by that love that spans eternity—we instinctively know how to help each other survive, no matter how dire the circumstances.

Windborne's energy continued to speak to me, answering all of the questions I had swirling in my brain:

I knew you were powerless and afraid inside your mother. I wanted you to know that you and your mother would be saved, that hope would find you. I knew that you would be in this arena one day. I was sent by the stars to send you that mes-

sage—and here you are.

He knew? He knew that my mommy and I would survive and be saved? The stars could send a messenger on this earthly plane? And to my dreams?

Yes, Windborne answered. *Now fly, dear Stardust! All of the love of the Universe and the trees and the sun and the moon and the stars are yours for all eternity!*

I suddenly felt a rush of energy in my heart and in my hooves that propelled me forward so powerfully that Kris had to pull back slightly on the reins to ask me to stay with her. She and I circled that arena like dragonflies in a field of clover, feeling the power of our moment.

I will always stay with you, I told Kris.

Her hands on the reins quivered in response—I could feel the pulse of the energy in her fingers right down to the metal bit in my mouth. The energy told me that she knew.

She then asked me to do a half-pass to "wow" the crowd. I loved doing the fancy advanced movements—I felt as if I had wings and could soar over mountaintops. Every muscle in my body had its job to send me gliding across the arena. My legs, my back, my chest, my hindquarters, my neck, were all synchronized with Kris who followed my movement with her elastic spine and relaxed legs. We were one celestial being; floating and flying.

We were the stars.

Then, Windborne's energy again reached my heart:

Fly, dear Stardust!

It was then that I realized that he and his rider were almost right behind me and Kris, also performing a half-pass. The four of us—horses and riders—were gliding forward and sideways with grace and strength.

"Here we have a spontaneous pas-de-deux, ladies and gentlemen!" the announcer said over the loudspeaker. "Aren't they beautiful!"

People clapped for us. I felt smile energy all around me.

All of us, we were the stars.

Then, magic happened—the other two horses and riders did half-passes and we became a quadrille. The applause became louder.

"All of these horses were rescued at the final hour, and look at them! Rescue a horse and discover brilliance!" the announcer exclaimed, inviting everyone to honor our stories of hope.

At the end of our demo, we all lined up in the center of the arena. The announcer introduced all of us to the audience, one by one:

"First, we have Lucky Charm, ridden by Lacey Roderick!"

Lucky Charm, a gorgeous bay like my mommy, trotted out to a thunderous applause. Lacey's face beamed like a comet on a clear night. She reached over the mare's neck to playfully rub her ears. Lucky Charm smiled with her large, kind eyes.

"Second, we have Ruby Slippers, ridden by Elizabeth Martin!"

Ruby Slippers stepped out like a great dancer taking center stage—she was the color of new copper penny with a brilliant white blaze that dripped down her lovely face. Her neck bowed elegantly as she lifted her knees in a perfect working trot. Her mesmerizing violet-brown eyes flashed and glimmered like the wings of a damselfly, reveling in her beauty and brilliance as if to say "look at me!"

The enthusiastic applause from the adoring crowd continued.

"Third, we have Windborne, ridden by John Russell!"

Windborne, snorting and proud, threw his powerful legs out in front of him to show the crowd his beautiful trot. He and his rider effortlessly circled the arena, then as they approached a corner, John sat deep in the saddle and asked Windborne to stretch his legs in an extended trot that drew awestruck-gasps from the audience. When he brought Windborne back to a working trot, John reached over to pat his horse's neck to thank him for a job well done. Windborne nodded his head ever-so-slightly to let John know that he had received his praise. The applause grew even louder.

"Fourth, we have Stardust and his rider Kristine Jenkins!"

I felt Kris's legs brush my sides and that was my cue to trot. I surged forward like a uncoiled spring and puffed out my chest to show the audience just how strong and brave I was. As I started trotting, the announcer added one last bit to my introduction:

"Stardust, I must note, was saved before he was even born. He and his mother were rescued from the kill pen with only hours to spare. Look at him now! Kristine trained him impeccably and now he is a dressage champion!"

We were the stars.

It is difficult for me to describe what happened next because the sound emanating from the audience was so deafening, so filled with elation—that my mind just focused on what I was feeling in that moment. My mind, body, and spirit were joined together to form a singular bolt of energy that filled the arena with a golden light. It bounced off the people in the audience and the other horses and riders as it raced through the air, touching everyone and everything with what I can only describe as love.

The canter

As I surged forward in my signature ground-covering canter, I felt the reins slacken, and then Kris's fingers giving my neck a quick, reassuring touch. She gathered the reins again as we slowed to a trot, eventually halting with my four hooves perfectly planted in the arena's soft, sandy footing.

I was brave as I felt the energy of my first friend, Magic, enfolding my being with a warm rush not unlike a sudden summer rainstorm. I silently thanked Magic, wherever he was at that moment, for always believing in me. For being my friend. For comforting me when I was scared. For showing me that through kindness, all things are possible.

And my mommy. She was there, too—right next to me all the while, matching my heartbeat. She was always, always with me—every day, every moment. She always, always loved me.

Kris bent her head and saluted the crowd. I nodded my head with hers. The crowd continued applauding for us, and some even stood up to celebrate us in a swirling joy of sound. All I could see and feel were smiles. Big, happy smiles.

"That's my boy," Kris said to me. Only I could hear her. Those words were only for me.

And I, a discarded horse, had inspired many that day to rescue a horse of their own. I, a discarded horse, had ignited a passion for saving lives. More discarded horses would be saved and be allowed to live full lives with purpose.

I was sent by the stars.

So, what can be said for the discarded? What can be done? Are we destined to disappear if no one wants us? If we were abandoned and betrayed? Are we obligated to give up, simply because we were thrown away? Is hope something that only exists for a select few?

No. A sad beginning does not mean we will have a sad ending. We have the power to change the story.

We can reach out and invite love and mercy into our hearts.

We can choose to be kind, even if the world wasn't kind to us.

We can cling to hope because hope is always present, even if you can't see it right away.

We can hold our heads high, and let our nostrils flutter in a rolling whinny and invite hope to hear us.

And the time we have—we can choose to live every moment with joy and gratitude.

We can choose to never let anything reduce us or steal our happiness.

We can show the world that we matter.

Chapter Twenty Two
The Moon is Always There

When Kris and I returned home that evening, the first voice I heard calling to me was Nala's.

I am so proud of you, Stardust!

Then, Tara joined in with her sweet soprano whinny:

You did it, Stardust!

Then, I heard my mommy whinnying to me from her stall in the lower barn, her sweet, small voice barely audible like a breeze through the branches of the pine tree, in the evening wind:

You have become the horse I always knew you could be, my dearest!

Her voice filled my being with a pale golden-pink light as I called out to her, my voice strong and loud:

I love you, Mommy!

Kris, pitchfork in hand, fluffed up the wood shavings in my stall—then topped off the water in my bucket and dropped sweet apple and carrot slices in my feed tub. I devoured them making smacking noises with my lips. Such delight!

"Good job, Buddy," she said to me as she smoothed out my forelock with her fingers. "You enjoy, you earned it. I will see you in the morning." Her voice—that rainfall voice—always offered me comfort and love.

Then Kris turned on her boot heel, left my stall, bolted my door, walked down the aisle, and slid the barn door shut for the night. Nala nickered at me from her stall. I nickered back.

The moon was nearly full and it delivered a shower of silvery beams through the barn windows as we shuffled around in our stalls getting ready to close our eyes and rest. Around the moon were dozens and dozens of stars glimmering and twinkling in the cobalt sky. The moon and stars could always be counted on. I always noticed them. I was named after those very stars.

And the moon. The moon was always there, even in the daytime. It lit up the night to let us know that hope was always present, holding us in its gentle grasp.

I dipped my head and cocked a back leg as I relaxed after the day's proud accomplishments, and prepared to slip into a deep sleep. I was so very tired—the day had been long and exciting, and now it was time to let go and rest. My eyelids were as heavy as steel horseshoes. I let them fall like curtains over my tired eyes.

Even as a grown-up horse, I could still recall my mommy's loving voice in my ears as she kissed me goodnight:

You are safe. You are loved. I will always be with you, my dear son.

I will now end my story here and leave you with this:

When you are frightened, look to the moon and let hope find you. Follow the kind, rainfall voice calling to you—trust that it will keep you safe. Let your heart be open.

Be brave, and always keep your face to the sun. The sun is the brightest star in our sky. It will lead you to where you are meant to be.

That is the amazing thing about stories: we can change the ending if the beginning was sad.

What will *your* story be?

You are the stars. Stretch your legs over the earth and discover how far you can go…

Afterword

Amanda was fifteen years old, and she was already an excellent dressage rider. She and her mother were eager to attend the demonstration of rescued dressage horses and arrived early at the venue to secure good seats. Amanda desperately wanted a horse of her own and even though her parents supported her equestrian passions, they wanted to be sure she was truly committed to the hard work required to keep a horse before they bought one for her. Amanda volunteered at her local barn to show her parents that she was serious. She mucked stalls, scrubbed buckets, swept the barn aisles, and cleaned tack after school and on weekends. Her hands were permanently streaked with saddle soap, and the pockets of her jeans always had shards of hay and horse treats in them. She was a true horse girl—she even offered to muck stalls on Christmas day so the barn owner, Heather, could have a day off.

She worked so much that she earned a free riding lesson each month. Amanda was proud that she was able to contribute to her riding education rather just having her parents pay every week. Amanda knew that in order to have something, you have to earn it and work hard. So she did.

That day at the demonstration, as she and her mother watched the graceful rescue horses doing their dressage movements, Amanda felt as if her heart felt would burst open with longing. The horses were grand and perfectly trained—she ached to ride all of them.

These horses are a dream, she thought as she watched all four of the horse and rider teams perform their half-passes and shoulder-ins.

"Look, there is Stardust," Amanda's mom exclaimed as a handsome, dark-bay gelding trotted by them, effortless and glorious. "The one who was born at Summerbrook!"

"There he is!" Amanda said, her voice rising with excitement. "Wow, look at him, Mom! He is beautiful!"

"He was the colt that Magic befriended, remember Heather telling you that?" Amanda's mother continued.

"That's him?" Amanda said with awe in her voice. "I think Magic would be so proud to see him today!"

Magic was the horse who taught Amanda all about being a horse girl. When Amanda was small, she sat on his back and gripped his copper-colored mane with her little fingers. It was then that she knew that she wanted to fill her life with horses. It was Magic who invited her into his equine family.

Magic seemed to be there, in that arena, at that moment. He was in Amanda's heart and his energy surrounded Stardust as he performed for the audience. The energy that twinkled all around Stardust held a coppery-red blush—and it let him know that his old friend was right there with him.

The demonstration ended with people on their feet applauding the beauty of the equestrian art of dressage. These horses, saved from terrible situations, had enchanted the crowd and filled the arena with a life-energy that had touched everyone's hearts. Stardust, in particular, stood out because of his great beauty, elegance, and kind nature. And that canter of his!

On the ride home, Amanda pleaded with her mother:

"I want to rescue a horse. I want my own Stardust. Please, may we do that, Mom? Please? And if not now, what can I do to work harder to make that happen?"

Amanda's mother smiled warmly, and nearly crying tears of happiness at her daughter's sensitivity, uttered the first thing her heart wanted to say:

"Yes. Yes, we can rescue a horse. There is a Stardust waiting for you. We will discuss this with Dad when we get home, but I am sure he will agree. You have worked hard; you have earned this. My goodness, you even gave up your Christmas mornings. Of course we can do this. We are both so proud of you,

Amanda."

Amanda exclaimed with all of the pent up excitement in her being of her dream finally realized:

"Mom! Thank you, thank you, thank you! Let's go as soon as we can, please? My poor horse is out there and he can't wait another day. He needs me, he is in a pen lonely, hurt, and scared…."

….

….the truck and trailer slowly makes it way up the Summerbrook Stables driveway. Inside that trailer, a thin, scared bay gelding whinnies out into the early evening air. His ribs poke through his dull coat, and his eyes are wide with uncertainty. Was he going to another Bad Place?

Where am I? he frantically wails through the bars of the trailer. Am I safe?

A chorus of whinnies from the Summerbrook horses answer him:

Welcome to Summerbrook! You are safe! Do not be scared!

The trailer comes to a stop, and Heather and Amanda unclip their seatbelts and exit the truck. Their work boots thud dustily on the ground—it had been a long drive but they are finally at Summerbrook with a young bay gelding who was in desperate need of their help. They had rescued him with only minutes to spare.

Heather approaches the trailer to unlatch it, then stops.

Amanda, she says, You lead your horse off the trailer. He needs you, not me.

Amanda, the courageous horse girl, smiles at Heather's gesture and hurriedly unlatches the trailer gate, lets it swing open slowly, and calmly walks up to greet her new horse. The frightened bay gelding reaches for her coat sleeve with his muzzle. She gently strokes his gaunt neck before clipping the lead rope to the brass ring on his brown leather halter, and says to him in the gentlest voice possible:

Easy, boy. You are home. Come with me.

The bay gelding's fear suddenly evaporates into the early evening air leaving a trail of gray mist that dissipates into the sky above. Amanda has an easy energy that lets him know that he is out of the Bad Place and that he will not be loaded onto the Bad Truck. She moves slowly and carefully and her voice is soft as the thrum of a hummingbird hovering over bee balm. Beyond the trailer, his keen nostrils capture the dusky scent of hay and oats. The aroma lets him know that happiness lives in this new place.

The bay gelding willingly follows Amanda off the trailer, pulling slightly on the lead rope—but not too much. He wants to find the food and bury his face in it, but he knows to be respectful of the nice horse girl leading him.

Good boy! Amanda praises him.

He is so thin, Heather observes. Poor boy. We will soon put him right.

Amanda reaches over and rubs the gelding's ears. He leans into her touch and lowers his head before exhaling loudly through his whuffling nostrils.

You are home, Starlight, Amanda says to her bay gelding as she scratches the itchy horsefly bites on his face and neck. The gelding feels safe enough to lower his heavy eyelids. He soaks up Amanda's kindness like bran in warm water.

Starlight, Heather muses, her eyes twinkling with remembrance. Sounds a lot like Stardust!

Yes, the great dressage champion who was born here! Since he inspired me to save a horse of my own, I felt it was only right, Amanda says with a broad smile.

Heather reaches out to give Amanda a quick hug as her mind fills with the memory of the dark colt with the star on his forehead. She had been present for his birth and had cheered him on as he took his first steps.

Stardust, the rescued champion, was born in one of her barns, safe and warm in a stall piled high with soft shavings and straw. The first human voice he heard was Heather's. Because of that moment Stardust only knew humans to be sweet and patient. As it should be for every horse.

Starlight, the rescued bay gelding, is to know this, too. He is thin, but strong. He is wary, but brave. He had been mistreated, but is now able to accept trust into his heart again. He knows that his horse girl Amanda will not discard him. He knows that she will always be there, until his last breath many, many years from this day.

There were many days still ahead filled with friends and purpose....

....That first evening in his new home, Starlight is able to rest his mind and his body for the first time in what seems like forever. The night is as quiet as a pine forest wrapped in snow. His water bucket and his belly are full.

The moon above glows with a chilly luminescence that covers the barn and the earth with a pale blanket. The stars dance in their illumination as they have done since before the birth of time.

The moon and the stars were always there offering the stillness of the night, and holding the promise of a new day. The bay gelding looks up at the winking stars and exhales long and deep, fully emptying his lungs of all of the worry he had held on to for far too long.

Starlight had once been discarded, frightened, and forgotten, yet that is not to be his destiny. His heart is finally hopeful. He can look forward and not be scared of what lies ahead of him.

As Starlight closes his eyes, he drifts off to a land of clover-blanketed hills and open fields. He dreams of green grass and yellow and purple wildflowers that smell like summer. Old friends await him in his dreams—they gallop alongside him and whinny their joy:

You are saved! You are saved! You are saved!

The bay gelding sleeps so deeply that he does not open his eyes again until the sky *turns rosy with the sunrise. The pine trees just outside his stall window watch over him as hope enters his heart.*

As he stirs in his stall, one word blissfully canters into his once-troubled mind:

Home.

Acknowledgements

It takes a team to make a book breathe. I am blessed beyond words to have the love and support of so many friends and family.

THANK YOU:

To my husband, best friend, and creative partner Steve Scanlon for his editing and designing magic. Thank you for saying 'yes' over thirty years ago.

To my readers Donna Dunbar, Cathy Cementina, and Keirsten Riccio for their honest and constructive feedback—and to Keirsten for her beautiful foreword.

To Anna Morales and Willow. All the love.

To my wonderful family for always cheering me on, especially my mother. I love you, Mom.

To my friends for listening and offering validation. This is no small thing. I am profoundly grateful.

To my cats Thomas and Timmy for being little glimmering starlights in my life.

To the memory of Pat Scanlon, Mark McPartland, and Maggie Kendis. Your energy continues to inspire my words and my art. You are never far from me.

To those who rescue horses and make fear disappear.....

....May the light of the Universe shine upon you always.

Gratitude.
Helen

The broken golden stars carried their message of undying love to the galaxies and beyond. I kept a few of the pieces in my heart for safekeeping. ~Stardust

Other books by Helen Scanlon:

My Horse, My Heart: The Morgan Horses of the University of Connecticut
The Great Red Horse: A Colt is Born
The Great Red Horse: A World Champion
The Great Red Horse: The Legacy
Dust and Determination: A History of UConn Polo
Because of a Horse
Lessons With Magic

www.helenscanlon.com

www.ingramcontent.com/pod-product-compliance
Lightning Source LLC
LaVergne TN
LVHW010614110826
845149LV00003B/906

* 9 7 8 0 9 8 9 4 1 6 8 7 0 *